Birds of a Feather

The Salt Sisters

Katie Winters

Chapter One

June 1993

The first time Rose saw Nantucket Island, she was twenty-one years old. In a cheap miniskirt and a baseball cap, she stood on the top deck of the Nantucket Ferry, hands around the railing, chin lifted. Tears drained her eyes and lined her cheeks, and her tongue was scratchy from dehydration. *But I made it,* she told herself as the soft northern breeze swept through her hair. *I'll never go back to Mississippi again.*

Back home, Rose had answered an advertisement in a newspaper. It read: **Good with kids? Hungry for an adventure? Contact us for the summer opportunity of a lifetime.** Although she'd never worked with children beyond her seven younger brothers and sisters, she'd called the number immediately. She pressed the phone hard against her ear to combat the demonically loud television her father played at all hours of the day. A woman with a prim voice answered, asked Rose a series of simple questions about her background,

1

and set up an interview. Rose learned later that the first woman was only a secretary, a first line of defense between potential babysitters and the Walden family. There were numerous interviews, followed by a meet and greet with the mother and the four Walden children. It was a shock to Rose that she'd gotten the gig. She'd never gotten anything in her life.

Rose had only a backpack and a small suitcase filled with essentials, mostly play clothes and swimsuits since the majority of her hours would be spent with the children. She carried these down the ferry ramp and out toward the ticket office. A chauffeur awaited her in a black hat and an all-black outfit that looked sweltering. His smile was brief and not warm.

"Good afternoon, Miss Carlson," he said. "How was your trip?"

Rose shifted her weight from foot to foot and watched him ease her dumpy-looking bags into the back of a sleek BMW.

"It was my first time on an airplane," Rose said finally, then cursed herself. *Don't let anyone know how green you are, even if it's true.*

"Welcome to the twentieth century," the driver said dryly. He opened the back door and gestured for Rose to enter.

Rose buckled herself in and crossed her arms tightly over her chest. She bit her tongue when asking the chauffeur what to expect from this spring and summer in Nantucket. She already guessed he wasn't the sort of man to look out for others, that his rank as "chauffeur" put him far above "family babysitter." Plus, he was in his forties or fifties and clearly wanted nothing to do with helping a twenty-one-year-old girl from the sticks.

I crawled out of my life, Rose reminded herself. *Nobody did this but me. I don't need his approval or his help.*

It shouldn't have surprised Rose that the Walden house was the biggest she'd ever seen in her life. Located in the exclusive and wealthy east Nantucket Siasconset, the house was like something from a sprawling epic about American wealth, with a west wing and an east wing, three walled gardens, a private white beach, and woods on either side, thick with oaks and maples and birch trees.

An iron gate unlatched itself and swung open, allowing the BMW to cut through and park in the driveway. Rose didn't wait for the chauffeur to free her. She popped out and stood in shock, arms hanging loosely. The mansion had to have a thousand windows. It had to have a zillion rooms.

Rose had shared a bedroom with her two sisters her entire life. She'd never known what personal space felt like. But the Walden children assuredly had separate bedrooms. Their hide-and-seek games were probably epic. Rose said a small prayer for her future self. *Please don't let the children be massive brats.* She'd hardly met them in passing: two girls, and two boys, all between the ages of four and ten.

Mrs. Audra Walden herself met Rose in the sitting room a few minutes later. This was a surprise. Rose had imagined herself diving right in with her tasks for the children. But Mrs. Walden wanted to take a moment to properly welcome her to Nantucket, serve her tea, and, of course, provide her with the numerous house rules that would govern the following three and a half months of her Nantucket stay. Rose felt like a woman in a fairy tale, caught in a tapestry of rules she couldn't comprehend.

"For one," Mrs. Walden said, "there will be no leaving the grounds unless it is your day off. We've hired you to work for us, and that work requires you to be here. There's plenty of woods, beach, garden, and house for you and the children here."

Rose nodded. Where else could she go? She didn't have a car. She didn't know her way around the island. It seemed like a silly rule.

"You will have one day off per week," Mrs. Walden said. "Usually, that day will be Tuesday, although that is apt to change based on our schedules."

Mrs. Walden removed a small book from the side table and passed it to Rose. In it, Rose found instructions and schedules for each of the four children: Evie, age four; Hamilton, age six; Kate, age eight; and Hogarth, age ten. Hogarth was an old family name, apparently. Rose had dug into the Walden family and discovered several other Hogarths going back six generations. According to the schedule, the two older kids had tennis and French lessons, while the two younger children were required to nap and make art. Every day was regimented. Rose was reminded of *The Sound of Music* and wondered if she would find it within herself to break beyond the Walden boundaries and fuel life and beauty into the children's lives. She imagined she wouldn't. She didn't want to get fired. She had everything to lose.

Mrs. Walden led Rose to the beach to discover all four children in their swimsuits. Evie and Hamilton kicked a soccer ball back and forth while Hogarth and Kate leaped over the waves. A large picnic of strawberries, baguettes, cheese, watermelon, and cured meats was spread across a blanket. A maid supervised them with her

4

hands on her hips and bucked away as soon as Rose arrived.

Rose thought, *They're my problem now.*

But that first day was magical.

As soon as Mrs. Walden disappeared inside to "make phone calls," the four Walden children surrounded Rose, captivated by her, asking question after question.

"Where did you come from?" Kate asked.

"I'm from Mississippi," Rose answered.

"Jackson," Hogarth said, raising his chin with pride at having remembered the capital.

"No," Rose said. "I'm from a tiny town called Carmack."

"Carmack," Hogarth repeated, furrowing his brow.

"You have a funny accent." Evie sniggered.

Rose smiled nervously. She'd expected them to tease her for her Southern drawl and had even tried to practice it out of herself. She'd run out to the fields and woods outside of the little shack where she'd been raised and whispered to herself in what she assumed was a "northern accent." But it was uncomfortable to speak like somebody else. She wasn't very good at it.

"Everyone speaks differently," Rose explained. "It depends on where you come from."

Evie pondered this for a moment and turned to her sister for confirmation. Kate nodded vigorously.

Somebody had taken Rose's bags for her upon her arrival, which meant she was at the beach without her swimsuit. Because she was wearing a tank-top and thick black underwear, she removed her skirt and went swimming with the kids, rolling through waves that felt so blissful and chilly and powerful. Hogarth and Hamilton cackled and leaped, splashing each other and their sisters.

Rose kept tabs on Evie and Hamilton especially, as Mrs. Walden had said they couldn't yet swim. At one point, Evie slipped her hand into Rose's, and Rose's heart pumped with gladness. *They already trust me,* she decided. *It's going to be a brilliant summer.*

Evening fast approached. The air chilled and cast soft blues and purples as it blinked across the horizon. Rose knew it was time to gather the children up and get them cleaned up and changed for dinner. She wrapped Evie in a thick towel as Hogarth and Hamilton continued to splash. Kate attempted to draw her hair into a pristine ponytail, clearly imitating her mother's professionalism.

That was when Rose spotted the black smoke on the other side of the woods.

Rose drew herself to full height. The thick, ominous smoke roiled through the evening sky. It smelled like chemicals and burning wood. *Is the forest burning?*

Suddenly, a helicopter approached overhead and circled the smoke.

"What's going on?" Hogarth demanded.

But what could Rose tell them? She didn't know herself. "Let's get inside," she said, scrambling to throw everything in the picnic basket.

The helicopter and the fire captivated the children, so much so that it took bribery and cajoling to get them down the stone path that led back to the house. Rose carried Evie on her hip, trying to keep herself from looking back at the fire. *What if we have to evacuate?* she wondered. *Should I get my things? Where is Mrs. Walden? Is this an emergency?*

Rose hurried the children through the side entrance, where they dutifully removed their shoes and went up the back staircase to their bedrooms and bathrooms, separate from their parents' bedrooms and bathrooms. Separate so that their parents only had to think about their children when they wanted to.

Rose paused at the base of the steps. Evie giggled as she erupted up the stairs after her brothers and sisters. Next came the sound of the shower; Hogarth, Hamilton, or Kate were already washing up. Rose had promised Evie she would help soon.

But Rose heard voices coming from down the hall. Two men and a woman. Mrs. Walden? Yes. Was one of them Mr. Walden? Were they talking about the fire?

Rose took a hesitant step away from the staircase. She knew better than to eavesdrop, but she ached to understand more about her surroundings. She sensed that Mrs. Walden would only tell her things on a need-to-know basis. She crept from the hallway into the dark sitting room. A door separated Rose and the three speakers.

"Of course, he can," Mrs. Walden was saying. "I just can't imagine he'd want to."

"The man's lost his way," one of the men explained. "I've never seen him like that."

"You don't think he..." Mrs. Walden breathed.

"Let's not get carried away," the other man warned. "We don't know anything yet."

"We know the house is unlivable already," Mrs. Walden pointed out. "Anyone with a nose can smell that." She cleared her throat. "Zachary, we'd be pleased to welcome you and your brother for dinner and drinks this week."

"I know he'll appreciate that," Zachary said. "Thank you."

"And thank you for letting us know." Mrs. Walden sighed. "We always assume Nantucket is the safest of all

7

the safe havens. Our children know it as heaven on earth. It's terrifying to know such things transpire just a forest away."

"It's hard to know how bad luck grows," Zachary said. "We must batten down the hatches and ensure nothing else threatens our magnificent community."

Mrs. Walden agreed.

What are they talking about? Rose furrowed her brow, listening harder. She understood that Mr. and Mrs. Walden weren't entirely on the same page and that Zachary's brother was somehow involved with the fire. *Zachary's brother has lost his way.* Was it his house? Had he burned it on purpose? Why would someone do that? For insurance purposes? Rose had grown up without two pennies to rub together, and it was often difficult for her to imagine the problems of the terribly wealthy. But she was surrounded by them.

Suddenly, the door between them burst open. A man she didn't recognize stood before her in a suit jacket and a pair of slacks, his hair mussed, his eyes red-rimmed and frantic. He looked at her with his jaw slack, then fixed his face into an arrogant smile—one that told her he'd *caught her doing something she shouldn't have.*

Mrs. and Mr. Walden squabbled behind him about something Rose couldn't understand anymore. Rose met Zachary's gaze and touched the wall beside her for support. She thought she was going to collapse. She thought he was going to tell on her immediately.

But he tilted his head. It took Rose a full ten seconds to realize what he hinted at. *Get out of here before they catch you.*

Rose tiptoed out of the sitting room and rushed up the staircase with the air of someone running out of that burning house across the forest. Her thighs screamed. *Why did he let me off the hook?* She marveled. But she didn't have time to question it further. Hogarth was out of the shower; Hamilton was refusing to bathe. There were tasks to tend to. It was only the first day in Nantucket. And the fire was clearly out of her control—and nothing that concerned her.

She decided to put it out of her mind.

Chapter Two

Present Day

The fact that Rose still ran forty-five miles a week at the age of fifty-two was nothing the Salt Sisters let her forget.

"I don't know how you do it," Hilary said during a yoga class in early August, flinging her head back as she spread her fingers across the mat. "My bones ache in the middle of the night if I walk too far on the beach. You're only three years younger than me!"

"It's just what I like to do." Rose laughed. "Trust me. If I could stay sane and not run, I would. But it's better than therapy. I swear."

The Nantucket Historic Society Yoga Center teacher gave them a look that meant *shush.* Rose giggled and re-focused on her stretch, drawing her arms out on either side and adjusting the way her weight sat on her hips. Beside her, Hilary was long and slender, evoking the elegance of her mother, the famous actress Isabella Helin. Rose's heart swelled with love for her. It had been twenty years since Rose had accidentally met Stella and Hilary. Twenty years since the narrative of her life had staggered off a cliff.

But Hilary had invited Rose into her home that summer. Rose had regrouped. She'd discovered her breath.

Not long after that, Hilary founded the Salt Sisters—a group of women who came together in grief; women who came together to support one another with open hearts and open minds. *No matter what happens.* By then, Rose had nobody. She ran to the Salt Sisters with her arms outstretched.

So many years later, Rose was dizzy with gratitude and had so many best friends in the Salt Sisters to call her own. Never could she have imagined her life going so well, especially after everything that happened.

Thirty minutes later, the yoga teacher said, "Namaste," and opened the doors to let them free. Rose and Hilary rolled up their mats and padded into the clear blue day. Rose had needed the stretch and strength-training. She'd been running herself ragged lately, stretching out her legs for farther and farther miles, opening her heart. *What are you running from?* she sometimes caught herself asking. But she didn't know. She just liked to put distance between herself and her home. She just liked to dig into the depths of her thoughts and figure things out.

Not that I'm any closer to understanding who I am or what I want, even at fifty-two.

Maybe that will be the journey of the rest of my life.

Hilary and Rose decided to grab lunch at a little Italian restaurant with to-die-for Mediterranean salads. It was just past one thirty, and the sun towered in the summer sky. Hilary was talking about her new boyfriend

—a man she'd met when she'd worked as a costume designer for an indie film. They had plans to cook tonight and watch a film, apparently. Rose felt her heart bruise. It was a consistent reminder of the fact of her life: she was doomed to live out the rest of it alone.

Not that Rose hadn't tried to date over the years.

Hilary poured her a glass of ice water and gave her a look that meant she could read Rose's mind. "What happened with that guy? What was his name? Roger?"

Rose snorted and raised the glass of water in a salute. "After some very light internet stalking, I figured out Roger has a wife and no fewer than *six* children."

Hilary winced. "That's the third guy this summer, isn't it?"

"The thing is, men used to be craftier about cheating," Rose said. "Now, it's insulting that he wanted to cheat on his wife with me, *and* he was unwilling to hide it. We're in the age of social media. We're in the age of Google. It took me ten seconds to figure out where he went to college, where he and his wife got married, and the names of his six kids."

Hilary sighed and rubbed her temples. Like many of the other Salt Sisters, both of them had been cheated on in the past. They agreed it was a perpetual metaphorical splinter, a pain they always felt in their big toe that they couldn't quite get out.

"Don't feel bad for me," Rose ordered Hilary. "You know how awful it feels to be on the receiving end of that."

"I know. I do." Hilary winced. "I just can't help but feel that somebody special is going to come sweep you off your feet."

"Unfortunately, he won't be able to catch me. I run too fast," Rose quipped.

After lunch, Rose said goodbye to Hilary and dipped into a local woodworker shop to chat with the owner about a potential sale. Charlie, the woodworker, knew Rose well and always stocked spare odds and ends for her, knowing she was apt to poke her head in and see what he couldn't use. Together, they piled fifteen pounds of wood into the back of her truck and secured it with pink bungee cords. Rose paid in cash at the register and chatted with Charlie about his recent sale—a gorgeous secretary desk he'd hand detailed for a very rich client.

"Can I take a peek?" Rose begged.

Charlie led her into the back so she could investigate "his pride and joy." Rose knew he'd charged the client eighty-five thousand dollars for it.

"She's coming to pick it up this afternoon," Charlie said sadly, walking a circle around the piece. "It's like somebody taking a piece of my soul out of my body and taking it home."

Rose puffed out her cheeks and tried to engage with every little unique detail on the staggering secretary's desk. Although she'd been among the Nantucket elite— and a dear friend of the wealthy Hilary Salt for twenty years—it was often still difficult for her to take herself out of her small-town Mississippi mindset and make peace with the fact that the wealthy threw their money around like that.

"Did she show you where in the house she's going to put it?" Rose asked.

Charlie nodded and placed his hands on his hips. "It's a gorgeous room. Soulless, though."

"It won't be soulless once this finds its home there," Rose assured him.

Something in the corner of Rose's eye caught her attention. She twisted back toward a bulletin board stretched across the wall in Charlie's woodworking room. Yellowed papers hung with photographs of some of Charlie's tremendous work over the years, plus photographs of Charlie and his new wife, Julia Copperfield, his high school sweetheart. On the far right was a larger pamphlet on which a picture of an old and crumbling house was printed.

Rose's heart seized with recognition. She was drawn to it. There, in front of the pamphlet, she read the listing: FOR SALE - NEEDS WORK. They wanted five hundred and fifty thousand dollars for it, which seemed outrageous for its state. But still. But still, she couldn't believe it was finally for sale.

She felt as though she was levitating.

Charlie came up beside her and followed her gaze.

"Who gave you that flyer?" Rose asked. Her voice shook.

"Julia hung it up," Charlie said, speaking of his wife. "She gets romantic about old, abandoned places like that. After it burned down when we were teenagers, we used to drive by and try to get in."

"But there were guard dogs," Rose remembered.

Charlie cocked his head. "I didn't realize you were already on the island by then."

"I'd just arrived when it happened," Rose said.

She didn't say, *It burned down the day I got here*. It was too weird. Too convenient.

"It must have been '92?" Charlie said.

"It was 1993," Rose said because the date was burned into her mind forever. "June 16."

Charlie whistled. "Good memory."

"Does your wife want to buy it? Is that it?"

Charlie laughed. "I don't know. Probably not. She has so much on her plate with the publishing company. I can't imagine she'd want to add a huge fixer-upper like that."

Rose's heart pumped.

"If only someone who was really good with materials like wood and stone could buy it and fix it up," Charlie said, giving Rose a side-eye and knowing look.

"Ha." Rose snorted.

"You should at least make an appointment to see the inside," Charlie urged her. "Maybe it isn't as bad as it seems?"

"Maybe." Rose swallowed the lump in her throat and stepped away from the pamphlet. *Don't you dare think about it,* she thought. *Put it to rest.*

But of course, the minute she returned to her truck, there was no question of where she was headed. Rose slammed her foot on the gas, blared the radio, and felt frantic and alive in ways she hadn't in years, decades. She hated the idea of "signs," but she couldn't escape the knowledge that that pamphlet had been one. A manifestation.

Rose drove past the old Walden Estate and cut back beyond the forest that separated the two properties. Sure enough, in front of the old stone mansion was a massive FOR SALE sign with a phone number matching the pamphlet in Charlie's workshop.

Nobody had lived at the property for many years by now, and it showed. The forest had begun to crawl toward the mansion, sprawling around it, flailing its limbs toward the cracked or glassless windows. The roof of the ancient gazebo along the wild stretch of beach had sunken in, and it looked as though the columns on the main house's porch were ready to crumble at any moment. *Who would ever want to buy this place?* Rose wondered.

The property itself was gorgeous, with nearly a quarter of a mile of private white beach—a beach that needed to be cleaned and cleared, but a beach nonetheless. If the house wasn't there in the first place, they probably would have demanded far more than the current asking price. The house was in the way.

Rose knew that whoever ended up with the property would ultimately have the house bulldozed.

Hunger spiked along Rose's tongue, but it wasn't traditional hunger. It was something else. An urgent desire for something. A need. Rose got out of her truck and imagined herself striding through the gate and opening the door. She imagined claiming space for herself in that old estate—that estate that still carried so many secrets within its crumbling walls.

There was still so much Rose didn't know.

There was still so much Rose craved to know.

But Rose had tried desperately to put these mysteries to bed for the previous thirty-one years. She'd felt doomed to never understand them. She'd felt at the mercy of time.

Rose stood there next to her truck. When the wind picked up and shifted tree limbs that shielded much of the property, a slice of sunlight came over her face and blinded her.

Nothing is stopping you from doing whatever you want, she suddenly thought.

Rose grabbed her cell and called her financial planner. She had a financial planner these days after being the

16

kind of woman who'd worked herself to the bone to get where she was. She'd never received a handout.

"Good afternoon, Becca," Rose said with an uncertain smile. "I have a proposition. It's up to you to tell me if I'm crazy or not."

"Uh-oh," Becca said. She was accustomed to Rose's crazy ideas. She was accustomed to advising her to slow down and think. "Let's hear it."

"I want to buy an old and historic house in Siasconset," Rose said. "I want to buy it and flip it and transform it into an iconic bed-and-breakfast or hotel." She grimaced. "Tell me I'm insane."

Becca laughed. "I'll run the numbers and call you back. Send the details?"

"It's the old Grayson Estate," Rose said, her voice shaking. "Five hundred and fifty thousand asking price."

Becca let out another bark of laughter. Rose wondered if she saw right through her. Or had Becca told her financial adviser too much about her past?

"There's never a dull moment with you, Rose," Becca said. "I'll call you back soon."

They hung up. Rose stood alone at the edge of a property that still seemed to whisper *I know all about you.* It terrified Rose. But it terrified her so much that she felt she had to shut it up once and for all. And the only way to do that was through ownership. It was suddenly and tremendously clear.

Chapter Three

June 1993

Rose soon discovered that babysitting for a wealthy family like the Waldens was akin to isolating yourself from the outside world. That first night, after the children went to bed, Rose sat by the window of her bedroom and gazed through the darkness, trying to make out some semblance of smoke from the other side of the forest. But the helicopter had come and gone; the fire had been put out. All the chaos of the early evening had faded. Even the floors in the Walden mansion beneath her were quiet, presumably with Mr. and Mrs. Walden hidden away somewhere, enjoying very expensive cocktails and preparing for bed. *Did they still love each other?* Rose wondered. Had they ever loved each other? It was sometimes hard for Rose to imagine that very wealthy people loved anything but the money they currently had and the money they planned to one day earn.

Rose had more or less concluded she would never

have money. The only wealthy lifestyle she would ever enjoy was like this—as a babysitter or a maid or some other assistant to a wealthy person. She would always be wealthy-adjacent or just plain poor on her own.

But that was okay. Especially now as she slid herself beneath the comforter of the gorgeous double bed upon sheets thicker and lusher than anything she'd ever slept on. She remembered an expression she'd heard once. Five hundred-count sheets? One thousand-count sheets? She didn't know what any of it meant, but she assumed that was what she dealt with now. A status of sleep that the poor were never allowed to understand.

She drifted off to sleep immediately and woke up at three thirty. Evie was at her door complaining of nightmares, and then Evie was in her bed, sprawling across her, rotating back and forth.

It amazed Rose that Evie had already trusted her enough to get into bed with her for comfort. Then again, Rose assumed that Evie had always known not to bother her parents with anything like that.

But what had Evie done before Rose got there? Had she forced herself through her fears alone—at the age of four?

Rose had known not to bother her parents with that kind of thing, too.. The little ones weren't welcome in bed with Mom and Dad; they took refuge with Rose. But Rose had never taken refuge in anyone.

Rose wasn't even sure if her parents really loved her. Maybe there wasn't enough love to go around when you had so many children and so little money.

It was easy to make excuses for her parents. Maybe that meant she loved them. Perhaps it meant she was foolish.

Sometimes she believed that having so many children

and so little money was selfish. But that was a topic for another day.

The first full day at the Walden Estate meant throwing herself through the set schedules of the four children and trying—and usually failing—to keep up. Evie was quite needy and sleepy; Hogarth was braggadocious and eager to regale her with the facts he'd learned from his various tutors; Kate wanted to do her makeup and paint her fingernails; and Hamilton just wanted to run, run, run as far down the beach as he could. Rose struggled to keep up with him yet respected his frantic energy, deciding that he was an eight-year-old in the way of all eight-year-olds. It didn't matter that he was wealthy. He wanted to get dirty. He wanted to be wild and get into scrapes.

But that first night left Rose exhausted and homesick. After a shower, she sat in her bedroom and tried to write in her diary. That was when she realized she hadn't asked about her phone privileges. When would she have a chance to ask Mrs. Walden about calling home? She hardly saw her. It seemed clear that invading her and Mr. Walden's personal space was a no-go. This was based only on her hunch and the facial expression of Zachary, who'd caught her spying that first night and decided not to tell.

Why? Rose was left to wonder. Were the Waldens so notoriously cruel that it was better not to open a can of worms when they were around?

Once or twice, Rose allowed herself to wonder, *Why me? Why did they pluck a girl from Mississippi and bring her here?*

It was Rose's fourth afternoon at the Walden Estate. Hogarth's tennis teacher had come and gone, and she and the four children were spread out on the beach, their hair flapping, salt water drying and leaving crystals across their tanned arms and legs. Evie shot up and down the beach, her feet flying so that white sand flashed out behind her, and Hamilton threw stone after stone into the water and watched them splash.

That was when Rose heard the voices coming down the walkway.

Rose turned to peer out at Mr. and Mrs. Walden plus two men who looked so similar they had to be related. Rose's stomach twisted with the realization that one of them was Zachary—the man who hadn't told on her for spying. The other one was his brother, then. The one who was involved in the fire.

The four of them evoked wealth and prosperity. They evoked summering in Europe and skiing and eating oysters or whatever else rich people did. They had nothing to do with Rose's entire existence, which made them like an entirely different species to her.

Evie went mad with excitement. "Mommy!" She rushed for Mrs. Walden and threw her arms around her. Mrs. Walden's smile was difficult to read. Was she pleased to see her children? Or was she acting pleased in front of the brothers?

She terrifies me, Rose thought now.

Rose had to assume Evie's sandy exterior wasn't entirely pleasing for Mrs. Walden, who always dressed immaculately. She watched Mrs. Walden do her best to brush the sand from her dress. She had no success.

But all at once, the four "adults" were on the beach with them. Mrs. Walden gathered her children in a line so that they could greet the brothers properly. They all knew them, but not well.

"You've grown like a bean!" Zachery said to Hogarth. Hogarth beamed proudly.

"When was the last time you saw them?" Mrs. Walden asked.

"It must have been last summer," Zachary said. "The barbecue?"

"That's right," Mrs. Walden said, clasping her hands. She flinched when she caught Rose's eye. "I nearly forgot. This is our new babysitter, Rose. She's from Mississippi."

"Mississippi!" Zachary's eyebrows went straight up.

"We thought it would be nice to introduce the children to different sorts of people," Mrs. Walden said.

Rose stung with resentment. *I'm a different sort of person. I'm poor. I'm an experiment for them.*

But then she reminded herself of where she stood now: this gorgeous landscape, the frothing ocean, the delicious food she ate all day long. *This is an experiment for me, too.*

"How do you like it up here?" Zachary asked.

"It's beautiful," Rose answered.

"Quite different, no?" Zachary said.

Rose smiled wider and turned her attention to Zachary's brother, who'd remained quiet. There was a strange intensity behind his eyes, an anger Rose guessed was related to the fire. His dark hair hung in glossy curls, and his large hands were in his pockets. He was maybe six-two or six-three and towered above his brother. Rose guessed he was slightly older.

"My name is Zachary," Zachary said, sticking his hand out, "and this is my brother, Oren."

Rose hadn't expected such a wealthy man to want to shake her hand. It was clear they'd come to the beach to meet the children, not the help. But she slid her hand into his and was surprised to find his grip firm and respectful.

Oren didn't stick out his hand to shake. But he caught her eye and gazed so intently that Rose's eyes filled with tears. She refused to look away. It turned into a game shortly after, with Rose eventually losing when Mrs. Walden asked her a question about Hogarth's lessons. Rose explained everything that had happened at tennis lessons, sparing details that made Hogarth look worse at tennis than Mrs. Walden wanted to believe. Rose already knew that being rich meant keeping some things to yourself. It was all about image.

"Who wants a cocktail?" Mrs. Walden suggested, clasping her hands together.

"We never turn down a good cocktail," Zachary answered. "What about it, Rose? Will you be joining us?"

Rose took a breath. Mrs. Walden's face transformed. One second, it belonged to a *beautiful and very good hostess,* and the next, it belonged to a *violent monster.* But soon, she smiled and said, "What a wonderful idea. Yes, Rose. Why don't you join us after you put the children to bed? I imagine you have all sorts of stories from Mississippi to share."

"We've never been there," Zachary affirmed. "We'd love to know more."

* * *

It felt nonsensical that Zachary wanted Rose to spend time with them. Rose tried to figure out his selfish reasons as she ran through her chores that night: reading two stories to Evie and Hamilton, making sure Kate brushed her teeth, and listening to Hogarth practice his French dialect as he drifted off. Ultimately, she decided that Zachary was the kind of rich person who wanted to manipulate situations and see how far his power could go.

But Rose was curious.

Rose's heart pounded. She returned to her bedroom to see if she had anything appropriate to wear but discovered nothing but a boring black dress she'd bought secondhand during a spontaneous trip to Jackson last year with her cousin. She'd spent no more than seven dollars on it and knew Mrs. Walden would see all the way through it, right down to its cheap details and bad stitching. But it was all Rose had. She buttoned it to her chin and brushed her hair, remembering the fire and ache behind Oren's eyes. *Oren hadn't said a word.* She wondered if he was mute. Or perhaps something had happened in the fire. Something that had affected his mental state so sensationally that he could no longer bring himself to say anything at all.

Rose discovered Mr. and Mrs. Walden with Zachary and Oren in the lounge. A vinyl turned and turned on the record player, and the speakers crackled with The Doors. The four of them were in separate chairs—Mrs. Walden on the chaise lounge, Mr. Walden in a black leather chair, Zachary on an identical leather chair directly opposite, and Oren all by himself on the sofa. The spot beside him was all there was available. Rose's blood pressure spiked at the idea of sitting so close to him. She'd have preferred Zachary, who seemed so kind, so eager.

Rose remembered Mr. and Mrs. Walden's sharp questions that first night. Had they thought Oren was involved in the fire somehow? That he'd caused it?

"Good evening!" Zachary was on his feet to greet her.

"Hello, darling," Mrs. Walden said. Her cheeks were flushed from cocktails. "We were just talking about you."

"Were your ears burning?" Mr. Walden asked.

Rose laughed nervously. Zachary crossed the room to mix a cocktail for her, something he said was straight from the Amalfi Coast and *to die for*.

"The girl doesn't know where the Amalfi Coast is," Mrs. Walden said. Her voice was syrupy.

Zachary gave Rose a sharp look, then said, "She knows where the Amalfi Coast is. Who doesn't?" He laughed. "Don't discredit this one. She's sharp as a tack. Look at her."

Rose offered a nervous smile, grateful that Zachary had decided to assume she knew where the coast was. In actuality, she had no idea. Geography hadn't been covered well at her high school. She could list most of the state capitals, and that was about it.

From where Rose sat with her cocktail, she tried to gauge Oren to figure out what he was doing there and what he'd been through that week. But Oren seemed uninterested in giving himself away. He hardly spoke. He hardly drank. Mr. and Mrs. Walden and Zachary were drunk at this point, gesticulating wildly through their stories. It felt as though Oren refused to play along.

"Tell us about Mississippi," Zachary urged when Rose was halfway through her cocktail. "We need to know about your life before Nantucket."

Mrs. Walden scoffed as though she couldn't understand why anyone would want to know about such a heinous place.

Rose stuttered and considered what she could possibly say.

"What was your house like?" Zachary pressed it. "What are your parents like?"

Rose imagined what her parents were doing right at that moment. It was nearly eleven, which probably meant they were drinking domestic beer and watching reruns on television. They'd probably gotten into some kind of argument that had mounted to such decibels that the windows had shaken in their panes and the little kids had wept in their beds. But they refused to get divorced. They couldn't afford it, for one. And for two, they probably knew they were two peas in a pod. Who else could stand them?

"My house at home is nothing like this house," Rose began, her voice shaking. "You could call them direct opposites, in fact."

"We had a private investigator take photos of the house," Mrs. Walden said, her words slurring together. "I can show them to you if you like."

Rose's jaw dropped with surprise. She imagined herself on the front porch with her little siblings, wrangling them and cleaning things up as a hot-shot private investigator circled the house with a hot-shot camera. *How dare they?* Rose thought.

Mrs. Walden giggled. "You can see how hot and bothered she is about it, can't you?" She put her hand on Mr. Walden's knee. "But how else could we trust someone with our babies?"

"We couldn't," Mr. Walden affirmed. "It was out of the question."

Zachary raised his eyebrows with surprise and glanced at Oren. "I wonder if Mother and Father ever did that with our governesses," he said quietly. "You must remember them, Oren. Don't you? The plump one who ran off with the plumber? The pretty young one who always made-up silly voices for our stories? What about the other one—the one who could ride horses?"

Oren looked genuinely uncomfortable. Suddenly, he was on his feet, with his hand over his chest and his eyes on the veranda stretching along the mansion's top level. He bucked for the door and opened it to walk outside, where he hung himself over the side of the veranda railing and gazed out at the black horizon of the Nantucket Sound.

Mrs. Walden got up swiftly to close the door behind him with a fluid motion, then turned to clasp her hands together and look at Zachary.

"He's been through a lot," Zachary reminded her. "Just this week, he's lost everything."

It took Mrs. Walden several seconds to fix her face, as though this deep into the night and into the cocktails, she'd lost full control.

"Of course," Mrs. Walden said. "I can't imagine how awful it's been."

"Can't imagine," Mr. Walden agreed, tossing back some of his cocktail. "You'll let us know when the funeral is, won't you? We really do want to support your family."

Rose furrowed her brow with surprise. Before she could stop herself, she breathed, "I'm terribly sorry for your loss."

Zachary's face broke into a strange smile. "Thank you, my dear. I'm sure that will mean a lot to Oren if he ever gets back inside and faces himself."

But there was no mention of who had died. Mrs. Walden changed the subject, and Zachary dove immediately into iconic tales that had transpired in faraway lands. There was no way of knowing if any of the stories were true. Rose allowed herself to drop into them anyway, imagining herself somewhere in the backdrop, on an Asian mountaintop or floating on a crystalline sea.

Not long after that, Mrs. Walden indicated it was time for Rose to return to her bedroom. They were done with her.

Throughout that time, Oren didn't flinch. His eyes remained on the horizon. *He'd lost everything.*

Chapter Four

Present Day

It shouldn't have been so easy to buy the Grayson Estate.

But with a bit of minor finagling from Becca, the financial planner, Rose left the real estate office with the keys just one week after she'd seen the flyer in Charlie's woodworking shop. A smile played across her lips. *I can still surprise myself,* she thought.

But Rose wasn't fully sure she wanted to step through the ancient doors of the Grayson Estate by herself—not without proper assistance. It was clear the property was damaged and potentially dangerous. She needed someone to do another thorough inspection to tell her where she could go and what she could do as she plotted and schemed her way to refurbishing it in time for next year's tourist rush.

Rose contacted Charlie first thing. She knew he had experience in that world, and he agreed to meet her at the Grayson Estate first thing in the morning.

He also said:

> I can't believe you bought it.

> ROSE: Call it a late midlife crisis.

> CHARLIE: Magical things come out of midlife crises sometimes.

> ROSE: Let's hope this is one of those times!

The Salt Sisters' group chat was all over the place about the news.

> HILARY: Tourism is gold around here. I think it's a brilliant idea.

> TINA: Isn't that place haunted?

> ROSE: It's haunted by the events of my life, but it's not haunted for anyone else. I don't think it is, anyway.

> STELLA: You don't sound totally convinced it's not haunted. Should we call the Ghostbusters to swing by, just in case?

> ROBBY: Didn't the Ghostbusters retire?

> HILARY: There has to be a new generation of Ghostbusters. It's the 21st century. Times are changing.

Rose giggled to herself, reading the messages out on the veranda of the home she'd bought and fixed up for herself going on fifteen years ago. The house was not far from Hilary's place, with an elaborate rose garden, quaint brickwork that reminded her of old-world German architecture, her fingernail crescent of white sandy beach, and plenty of room to roam around. She'd always lived here alone—

although there had been a boyfriend in her mid-forties who'd nearly moved in before they'd both gotten cold feet and separated. Rose thought of him fondly, though they hadn't spoken to one another in many years at this point. *Another chapter of my life,* she remembered. *Another thing I had to say goodbye to.*

Rose had been flat-broke when she'd first met Stella and Hilary in 2004. Hilary's offer for her to move in had enlivened her up to a point. It also reminded her of the definition of her life: other people would always be wealthy. Not her.

But that had changed. Miraculously. Insanely.

Set on remaining in Nantucket no matter what, Rose had moved into a quaint apartment after leaving Hilary's place and put herself to work. She'd waitressed; she'd worked at the movie theater; she'd scrubbed floors and tutored high school students and paid every single one of her bills on time.

But it wasn't till she discovered her artistic side that the money rolled in.

Rose had always enjoyed making art and using her hands. During her stint at Hilary's, she'd helped Hilary paint several rooms in the house and gave advice on carpeting, drapes, and artwork. Hilary had said at the time, *You have a sharp eye for detail, Rosie.* Rose had brushed it off.

Two or three years after her stay with Hilary, Rose discovered a canvas on sale at a secondhand place and bought it for three bucks. Paints were more complicated to come by, but she eventually wrangled some from an acquaintance of Hilary's who'd taken up painting briefly before abandoning it for what he called his "true hobby," which involved partying on sailboats.

That first painting had been relatively conservative in form and function. Rose had selected the Nantucket lighthouse as a subject and spent a good two weeks perfecting it. Not long after, she showed it to Hilary, who immediately set her up with an art dealer named Oriana Coleman. Oriana sold the painting for what Rose took to be a small fortune. *Ten thousand dollars.* Oriana urged her to paint more.

Rose did.

In fact, Rose spent the next twelve years exclusively painting her way across three hundred and sixty-two canvases. She painted anything that came into her head: lighthouses and beach bluffs and ancient houses, majestic horses, pancake spreads, and children holding ice cream cones. A few very rich people reached out to her to ask to have their portrait painted because the very rich were always narcissistic. But Rose didn't mind. She profited off their narcissism. More than that, she adored painting portraits, digging into the soul of the person and seeing them for who they were.

It was with this cash that Rose could purchase this property along the water. With this artistic name, she could bounce from painting as a medium to something far more adventurous: sculpture.

Now, Rose abandoned the veranda and padded downstairs to her studio. The studio was the biggest room of the house, with walls twenty feet high and a massive window that echoed back to the view of the Nantucket Sound. A chandelier twinkled its lights from the ceiling.

Rose had assembled Charlie's spare wood in the

corner of the room. She had plans for it, but it would have to wait till after she finished her current piece—an all-stone abstract sculpture she'd already sold for more than half a million dollars to a friend of a friend of Hilary's famous daughter. *"Ingrid's friends cannot believe she has a connection to you,"* Hilary told Rose after Ingrid returned to her life. *"They can't believe they have an exclusive connection!"*

It was often strange for Rose to remember the mighty twists and turns of her life. *How did I get here? How did any of this happen?*

But it had.

Rose wasn't immune to impostor syndrome. But she was getting better and better at pushing it aside, which counted for something.

* * *

Charlie agreed to meet Rose at the Grayson Estate the following morning at eight thirty. He came with a few members of a local construction crew, all of whom wore hard hats and boots with inch-thick bottoms.

Rose led the men through the grounds of the Grayson Estate and up to the stone structure. A stone porch remained with those questionable pillars and led up to a crooked doorway that looked as though it had been rattled with an earthquake. The construction guys told Rose to hang back and wait while they entered the house. Rose resented being told to remain. But she also hadn't brought a hard hat and was wearing a pair of canvas shoes. *Rookie mistake,* she thought now as she wrung her hands.

It was a chilly day, lower sixties, and the wind rolled off the Nantucket Sound and swatted her curls around her face. She cupped her elbows and gazed at the forest separating this stone fortress from the Walden Estate. When was the last time she'd been there? It must have been the day she quit.

The Walden Estate was still owned by the family, of course. Rose knew that the children returned to the estate every summer with their own children and probably with their own babysitters. She wasn't sure if either of the elder Waldens were still alive, although they weren't so old. Mid-sixties, maybe seventies. It was hard for Rose to envision them as anything but their gorgeous and well-dressed and beautiful selves.

Rose grabbed her phone and Googled their names but found nothing beyond a few articles about their "magnanimous contributions to Yale, Harvard, and Columbia." Rose had heard a rumor that they'd only sent these funds to ensure their children would secure beautiful futures at an Ivy League university. She'd heard another, darker rumor that they'd had to send even more funds to Yale after Kate or Evie had gotten into trouble. Rose was pretty sure it involved vandalism, although most journalists knew to keep hush-hush about the matters of such a prosperous family.

It wasn't hard for Rose to imagine any of the Walden children getting into trouble. It was hard to imagine that they'd ever grown up fully, though. Evie had been four in 1993, which made her thirty-five this summer. That put Hogarth at forty-one!

Rose shivered. Time was a slippery thing. Did they remember her? She'd only worked for the Waldens that summer and autumn back in 1993. It stood to reason that their memories of her had been stamped out with those of other babysitters and governesses. Rose wasn't special.

Rose googled Hogarth and discovered he'd become a mega-millionaire in his own right—with initial help from Daddy's millions, of course. Hogarth had founded and sold several million-dollar companies on his own and peered out from LinkedIn photographs that made him look like a prosperous professional. A bit of online digging made it seem like he'd divorced his first wife and married his secretary, but it was difficult for Rose to get the full story based on a few clicks.

Not long after that, Charlie called her name. "It's all clear! Come on through!"

Rose's throat was so tight that it was difficult to breathe. She shoved her phone into her pocket and delicately went up the stone steps.

How many times had she wondered about this place? How many times had she begged to come inside?

Now, here she was on the precipice. And she owned it! Nobody could tell her to turn away!

The place was just as haunted-looking as the Salt Sisters suspected. After the fire, the Graysons had done very little to clean the place up and had even left many of their once-immaculate items lost in the debris of stones, ash, and fallen wood. But because the old house was built with stone and iron, the foundation was solid. It meant it was rife for Rose's visions for refurbishment.

Maybe Rose would even hang a photograph in the foyer of what the house had once looked like—before and after the fire. Maybe she'd stitch the story of the house into the advertisement for the bed and breakfast.

Rose followed the sound of Charlie and the construction workers' voices and discovered them at the edge of what had once been a ballroom-dining room area. Miraculously, the dome of the room hadn't collapsed during the fire, although Charlie was fearful about what would happen once Rose attacked it with her "plans."

"If you want to keep the original roof, it needs to be stabilized first thing," Charlie told her. "There is no walking through this room under any circumstances until that happens."

Rose saluted him. "Roger, captain."

Charlie rolled his eyes. "I'm serious. If this falls, there's no getting out of the rubble."

Someone had painted the entire map of the stars upon the dome ceiling. It seemed outrageous that they were still visible, especially long after the fire, as the structure had sat here abandoned and without care for thirty-one years. But there they were: a splendorous array of the Big Dipper, Sagittarius, Aquila, and Centaurus. Rose's eyes filled with tears. She'd imagined the place to be specific, detail-oriented, and beautiful, but this was beyond her wildest dreams.

"Do you remember the rumors that went around about the fire?" Charlie asked now.

Rose cast him a look that meant *duh.*

Charlie laughed and snapped his hand across his thigh. "Wait a minute. I can't believe it's taken me so long to put this all together."

Rose's heart pumped. He'd figured it out. But hadn't Rose wanted him to?

You can't leave anything in the past, not in Nantucket. Everyone in Nantucket remembers everything. Collective memory is a terrifying thing.

The construction workers looked at Rose with buggy, curious eyes.

Rose rolled her head in a circle and considered whether or not to explain herself.

Finally, she came out with a weak, "I knew the man who owned the house when it burned down."

The construction workers continued to look at her, waiting for another layer of information that wasn't coming.

Rose didn't want to show all of her cards. Not yet.

Charlie gave her a look that meant: *Someday, you're going to tell me the entire story.* But Rose couldn't imagine speaking it aloud.

Charlie clapped his hand on her shoulder and beamed. "Why don't we give the construction crew a few days to go through the rest of the house? It's massive. They can stabilize things for you—things like those pillars outside, those walls."

The construction worker bobbed his head. "I want to bring another guy in to check out these roofs."

Rose could hardly believe she was having this conversation. She'd never dreamed she'd ever see the interior of the Grayson Estate. But here she was, enraptured in the daydream of a place she'd thought lost to time.

She was a part of that time, in a way, she thought now. She owed patience to the old place. She owed it artistry and hope so many years after it had been abandoned.

Chapter Five

June 1994

Rose couldn't help it. That night, long after she'd been dismissed to her bedroom upstairs, shivery from cocktails, she lay awake and stared through the dark, thinking about the mysterious Oren and the strange Mrs. Walden and the at-times vivacious Zachary, whose personality seemed to turn on a dime. Never had she encountered people like this in Mississippi. Never had she felt a sinister underbelly, as though the things people said could never be taken as the full truth.

The biggest curiosity, of course, was Oren and his "loss." There had been mention of a funeral before Rose had said, "I'm sorry for your loss," and Oren had abandoned the lounge for the surging darkness outside. Rose guessed someone had died in the fire. It stood to reason nobody had told her. Her life was a steady stream of children's needs. Her life was meant to fade into the background and do what needed to be done.

But two days later was Rose's first day off.

Rose woke up that morning at the crack of dawn. Evie was sprawled out beside her, as usual, her thumb tucked between her lips, her face still chunky with baby fat, and her eyes shifting dreamily behind their lids. Rose decided to carry Evie back to her bedroom so she could get a head start on her day. It was the first day that belonged totally to her. She had yet to strategize. But she knew she didn't want to spend a lick of time babysitting—not even to tend to Evie when she woke up.

Rose tucked Evie back into bed, then tiptoed down the hall to shower and change into a sundress with yellow flowers. When she emerged, the clock in the hall read seven ten. She decided to go downstairs to the staff kitchen to have coffee and maybe grab a snack. Maybe she'd see the housekeeper, Miriam, somewhere. Miriam was the stand-in babysitter today. Rose wanted to warn her about the rash on the back of Hogarth's legs. She wanted to remind her that Kate's complaints about her teeth had already been dealt with; Kate had a dentist's appointment next week.

Downstairs, Rose sat outside with a mug of coffee and watched the waves roll onto the white sand. She felt relieved and free in a way she hadn't since she'd arrived, as though she'd just gone through a great trial and emerged victorious on the other side. *In the future,* she told herself now, *I'll have so many days off. I'll work for myself. I'll be the one to say if I work or if I don't.*

This felt laughable, of course. Nobody in her class made their own schedules. They took what they could and made money as much as possible.

Miriam emerged with a stern smile and a nervous

glint in her eye. "What are you going to do for your day off?"

Rose stretched her arms over her head. "I was just thinking about that."

Miriam sipped her coffee. It was clear from the outset that she didn't really like children, that she'd taken this "extra day with the kids" with disdain and annoyance. But she didn't let that annoyance shake off on Rose, for which Rose felt grateful.

"I'd like to see more of the island," Rose admitted. "Since I'm not allowed to leave the grounds during the workday."

"Why don't you ask Baxter to drive you in?" Miriam suggested, speaking of one of the staff members in the kitchen. "He's headed to the market in fifteen minutes."

"How will I get back?"

Miriam made a face as though *getting back* was beyond her.

Rose decided she didn't care. She leaped up and hurried back to the kitchen to discover Baxter in his white apron, making a list of groceries on a pad of paper.

"Let me guess," he said now with a warm smile. "You want a ride to town?"

"Am I so transparent?"

"All the babysitters want a ride to town every once in a while," he said.

Rose's heart sank. *Does it mean he wants to say no?*

"Count yourself lucky," Baxter declared. "I didn't like the last babysitter much. I didn't always say yes. But you? You haven't made me angry yet."

Rose giggled, sensing he was teasing her. "Let me know how to stay on your good side."

"Just keep the Walden kids happy," Baxter said. "If they're happy, they're out of my way." He winked.

Rose sat in the passenger side of Baxter's little pickup with her purse on her lap and her hair tied in a still-damp knot on her head. Baxter was still out in the driveway, having a conversation with a guy there who was supposed to repair one of the Waldens' luxury vehicles. They chatted with each other like they knew each other.

Baxter cleared it up when he got in the car. "Tiny island," he said. "We all know each other."

Rose's heart swelled. The idea of a tiny island where everyone looked out for each other spoke to her sentimental side.

"Do the Waldens know everyone, too?" she asked as the truck chugged down the road.

"Let's put it this way. They only know the people they *need* to know," Baxter said with a barking laugh. "Everything is about appearances with them."

Baxter shot Rose a look that meant *if you tell anyone I said that, you're done for*.

Reading his mind, Rose said, "Don't worry. I don't have anyone to tell."

Baxter's face broke into a smile, and he turned up the radio to play a song from the seventies, one that Rose's father liked. She was pretty sure it was by Deep Purple. She felt a strange pang of homesickness, imagining that thick-as-milkshake Mississippi heat, the air conditioner that was never strong enough.

Baxter parked in the lot by the market. Rose considered asking him how she could get back but then reminded herself of Miriam's eye roll and decided she'd figure it out herself.

"Thanks for the ride," she said. "See you later?"

"Enjoy your first day off. The island can be a magical place. I hope it extends its arms to you," Baxter said.

Rose hurried away from the market with the eagerness of Evie on the beach. It was just eight in the morning, but plenty of tourists were outside, sipping iced coffee, tilting their heads to catch morning rays, or reading newspapers.

Rose wandered to the edge of the harbor and watched the sailboats rock gently against the docks, clasping and unclasping her hands. She was vaguely hungry. She checked the cash in her wallet to discover just eight dollars. It was funny; she hadn't been paid yet. But being in the confines of the Walden Estate meant never really considering that money was required to purchase things. The children's food appeared in the cabinets and fridge. The children's beds were stripped, and the sheets washed. Money was invisible and ever-present.

Did Rose really need money to have a good day off? She decided she didn't.

She started at the beach because it felt appropriate. She'd packed a book and laid out in her swimsuit, reading and eavesdropping on the tourists around her. A husband and wife had recently married, arguing about whether they should move to the suburbs of New York City or remain in the city.

"I told you from the beginning," the wife was saying, "I want children."

"That doesn't mean we have to abandon our entire life," the husband blurted. "We have friends in Manhattan. We have a gorgeous apartment. We have the parks and the studio and the..."

"We need to think about our baby's future," the wife shot back. "You weren't raised in a city. Neither was I!"

Rose soon tired of the fighting and decided to walk farther down the beach.

That was when she heard the wife declare, "Look! You made such a scene. You're ruining the beach for everyone else."

"I didn't start this conversation," the husband pointed out. "You did."

The beaches near the Nantucket Historic District weren't as beautiful as the beach at the Walden Estate. But Rose had that kind of beauty to look at every single day of the week. Now, she indulged in people-watching, in smelling fried fish and french fries and churning ice cream. Time was moving too quickly; she wanted to grab onto it and own it. It was already noon when she decided to sit down for a coffee and a sandwich for four dollars—half of what she had.

She'd selected a little diner just off the main strip of the beach. It sold easy and quick fare for cheap prices, mostly to locals who didn't want anything to do with the tourists. The locals were not wealthy like the Waldens. Based on the few conversations Rose overheard, she guessed they were fishermen, restaurant owners, shop owners, or tour guides. A few of them spoke about the "approaching big tourist season" with the air of a coming hurricane.

It intrigued Rose. It made her understand the density of this island. It housed so many different types of people.

There was an abandoned newspaper at the table beside Rose. She decided to grab it and read a little about the local news as she nibbled on her sandwich.

Local sports were just the same as in Mississippi: essential to the tapestry of the community. A style section showed photographs of tourists and locals alike in outfits that "showed their personalities and suited the 1993 style." There were wedding and graduation announcements, and announcements were made that various eighteen-year-olds were off to Yale, Harvard, or Princeton. Rose inspected the photographs of these handsome and beautiful and wealthy children, wondering what it was like to be born and have the world handed to you. Evie, Hamilton, Kate, and Hogarth had that, too. Their futures were bright. When they reached the pinnacle of their successes, nobody would be around to share the stories of Evie crawling into Rose's bed after a nightmare or Hamilton kicking and screaming when Rose told him he couldn't have any more dessert.

Kids are the same everywhere, she thought now.

That was when she saw the obituary.

NATALIE GRAYSON: May 11, 1967 - June 16, 1993

Alarm bells rang in Rose's ears. *She died in the fire.*

The photograph beside the obituary featured a beautiful woman with soft and ethereal hair and big and dreamy eyes. She wore a black dress with a high collar.

The obituary was simple. It read:

Natalie Grayson (née Quinne) passed away last week on the island of Nantucket. She is survived by her husband, Oren; her brother-in-law, Zachary; her parents, Hannah and Peter Quinne; and her brother, Dean. A private memorial service will be held June 24 at the Nantucket Angelic Gardens. In lieu of flowers, please donate funds to Natalie's

favorite charity, The Children's Cancer Research Association.

Rose read and reread the obituary and leaned back against the cushion with her arms crossed over her chest. Oren had lost his wife; Zachary had lost his sister-in-law.

But why had Mrs. Walden, Mr. Walden, and Zachary spoken as though Oren had set the fire himself?

And why had Oren agreed to stay with the Waldens during this time of grief?

Rose was stumped.

"How are you doing, sweetheart?" The fifty-something server with the ketchup-stained apron returned to refill her coffee. "Can I get you anything else?"

Rose coveted the pie in the rotating glass case but wasn't sure she wanted to give up her precious money quite yet. The day was still young.

Rose pointed at Natalie's photograph. "Do you know what happened?"

The server's face transformed and turned the color of paper. Her eyes flashed back and forth.

"You don't know?" the server asked.

"I'm just visiting the island," Rose said, searching for a lie that would get her more information. "But I used to know Natalie back in high school."

The server's eyes welled with tears. "You poor darling!"

A few other regulars tilted their heads and bodies, eager to get in on the conversation.

"She says she knew Natalie?" a fisherman asked, adjusting his black salt-encrusted hat.

The server nodded furiously.

"We were close when we were teenagers," Rose

offered, her face flushed. "We lost touch. I had no idea she was in Nantucket in the first place."

"You want my opinion?" the server muttered. "I think her husband had something to do with it."

A few others in the restaurant bowed their head in agreement.

The fisherman said, "I met her when she first got to the island. Beautiful girl. So smiley and happy. But the next time I saw her, she looked through me like I wasn't there at all. It was like he'd done something to her. Poisoned her."

Rose remembered Oren's dark face; those penetrating eyes seemed to see through her.

"Why would somebody burn his own house down?" Rose asked.

The server laughed nervously and wiped her palms on her apron. She looked at Rose as though she were the most innocent of all God's creatures.

"Oh, honey," the server said. "You have a great deal to learn about the wealthy, don't you?"

"Don't let her learn," the fisherman barked. "Nothing good comes from that kind of learning."

A family of four entered the diner after that, and conversation about the chance of murder in Nantucket filtered out. Rose was left to ponder alone. But a few minutes later, the server brought her a pie with ice cream "on the house," smiling sadly, reminding Rose that she'd just *lost her friend, Natalie.*

"Take care of yourself, honey," the server told her after she left that afternoon. "There's no telling what big, bad wolves are out there waiting for you."

Chapter Six

Present Day

Rose felt more at home in her studio than any place on the planet. There in the paint-dappled and ragged artist apron she'd bought twenty years ago, she stepped away from her stone sculpture, snapped her hands on her hips, and declared it *finito*. She couldn't wait to show it off, which was why she decided to invite all of the Salt Sisters over for dinner and drinks that night to celebrate.

She just had to send a text.

Then she had to go grocery shopping.

Everything is falling into place, she thought as she got herself ready to go, jumping into the shower and heading out to her car, her grocery list typed into her phone, her heart on her sleeve.

Had Rose peeled back through time to tell her twenty-one-year-old self that she actually enjoyed cooking now, she was sure her previous self would say, *That's impossible.* But it was true. Now that Rose's time was her

47

own, and nobody had told her where to be, what to do, or how quickly to do it, she loved spending hours in her kitchen, slicing and sautéing and roasting and baking. She loved the look on her friends' faces when she showed off a new recipe.

Her favorite thing to do in the kitchen was add a bit of Southern cooking flair to her recipes. A bit of spice they didn't understand around here. It was a way to honor her parents and that world she'd crawled out of. It was a way to remind herself of what she'd lost and what she'd gained.

Hilary and Stella got to Rose's first that early evening. They brought chilled chardonnay and plenty of questions about Rose's new project with the Grayson Estate. Stella looked captivated by her, as though she couldn't believe she'd taken this plunge after everything that had happened.

"It's like you want to play with fire," Stella said, swirling her glass of wine in the kitchen sunlight.

Rose waved her hand. "I swear, all the ghosts are gone. Or they're *mostly* gone." She laughed. "Charlie has a few friends in construction. They're in there now to really make sure everything is sound and ready for a big refurbishment. To make sure it's *safe* for me. The last thing I want is to get buried under some rubble in that so-called haunted house."

"Look at her," Hilary teased. "Her eyes are bigger than saucers."

"But you should see what was left behind after the fire," Rose gushed. "I mean, so much was damaged, obviously. But there's enough leftover antiques and artwork to blow your mind. The minute Charlie gives me the all clear, I'm going to drag you both in there."

Stella's eyes clicked with intrigue.

The other Salt Sisters arrived after that, each with wine and cheese and different perfumes, blowing through the kitchen with kisses and vibrant hellos. Rose fell into easy conversation, answering questions about the Grayson Estate, asking about husbands and boyfriends and work appointments. When a hush fell over the kitchen, Rose announced it was time to go to her studio and look at what she'd been working on.

"Let's do it!" Hilary cried.

Rose led her Salt Sisters into the studio and lined them up, watching their faces intently, trying her darnedest to comprehend what they felt when they looked at it. This piece had lived in her mind for months now. This was the first time she was showing the sculpture to anyone. She was delirious with excitement.

But each of the Salt Sisters' faces were dry and loose, as though they were confused.

Rose's heart lurched. *They don't like it. How could they? I've worked so hard on it. I've put my heart and soul into it.*

Rose twisted around to look at the sculpture herself.

But the sculpture wasn't there.

Rose's heart thudded. "What?" she gasped, clenching and unclenching her fists. "What the heck? Where is it?"

"Is it this one?" Ada gestured toward a stack of stones off to the right.

Rose ignored her and blasted across the studio. Was it possible she'd moved it elsewhere? But no. The sculpture was more than two hundred pounds. She could not move it without moving the flatbed upon which she'd built it. And the flatbed was gone, too.

I would have remembered moving that. I would have remembered asking someone to come pick it up.

What happened?

"This can't be," Rose muttered. "I don't understand."

"Was it stolen?" Hilary rasped.

Rose heaved forward and gripped her thighs. The world spun. Someone ran upstairs to fetch a glass of water, and Hilary put her hand on Rose's back and ordered someone else to call the police.

"It's a misunderstanding," Rose continued to sputter, as though that would make this mess go away.

Hilary bent down in front of her and made a face that reminded Rose of those days twenty years ago when Hilary had been her refuge, her only friend. Hilary cupped Rose's hands in hers and breathed, "Let's go upstairs where it's more comfortable. Okay?"

Rose felt like a child. Hilary guided her upstairs and stationed her in the shade on the veranda with a glass of wine. Dinner was nearly ready, but Rose felt no itch to go tend to it. Ada and Robby ran off to finish it, which was a real shame. The final touches were what mattered on the dish because they were Southern-inspired. Robby and Ada wouldn't know to do them.

Some things are more important than dinner, Rose thought dully.

Hilary and Stella sat on either side of Rose. Rose felt her heartbeat through the veins of her forehead.

"The cops say they'll be here soon," Stella said.

Rose flared her nostrils and filled her mouth with wine.

"Who else have you told about the sculpture?" Hilary asked now.

"All of you," Rose said. "But that's all."

Hilary pressed her lips together. "You'll have to talk to the client. Maybe they know something?"

Rose's heart seized. "Do you think they had it stolen to get out of paying the last installment?"

"Anything is possible," Stella said. "But most artists have their studios elsewhere, don't they? Who else knows you have your studio at home?"

Rose gestured vaguely. "All of you."

"And others, surely," Hilary said.

Rose sniffed. Maybe she'd mentioned her at-home studio somewhere in an interview. The internet was rife with information about her "artistic" life.

I'm a wealthy person now. I'm a wealthy person whose public information is out there for the taking.

Hilary snapped her fingers. "What about your video footage?"

"Right," Stella said, nodding urgently as though this would finally solve everything.

Rose winced and burrowed herself into the cushions of the outdoor sofa.

"Don't tell me you didn't get the camera fixed." Hilary grimaced and gave Rose a look that made her think of Mrs. Walden.

Maybe when you're born wealthy, you will learn how to make that face, Rose thought.

"It slipped my mind."

Rose's security video camera had stopped working last autumn, and Rose had had it on her to-do list practically *forever* to fix it. But she was far from the wealthiest person in Nantucket; she was far from the wealthiest person in the near vicinity. Rose had self-made wealth, which was never as staggering as inherited wealth.

It wasn't that the thieves had taken anything else.

They'd only taken her sculpture. They'd decided to hit her where it hurt.

Oh, it hurts so much.

It felt as though someone had carved out a piece of Rose's soul.

The police arrived shortly after that to take a statement. Rose showed them photographs of the sculpture and told them what she was selling it for. The police looked vaguely flabbergasted although they were surely accustomed to hugely expensive pieces of modern art in Nantucket.

I used to be one of you! Rose wanted to tell them, perhaps as a way to get them to help her even more. But she knew that once she'd crossed the boundary between the wealthy and the not, she'd ceased being one of them so much that they would never recognize her as one of them.

Well, they would probably recognize her if she lost everything again. But they'd also call her *stupid* for losing her wealth once she'd earned it.

Catch-22, she thought now.

One of the cops was a man Rose vaguely recognized from somewhere. It was almost as though he'd lurked in the outer edges of her dreams, as though she'd seen him thousands of times at the grocery store and never remembered saying hello.

The cop's name was Sean Slagle. He was broad-shouldered and dirty blond with a thick mustache above his upper lip and a way of looking Rose directly in the eye when he spoke to her.

"You're the woman who just bought the old Grayson Estate," he said, tapping his pen against his notepad. He said it as though he'd just solved a major riddle.

Rose nodded and searched his face for some clue of who he was or where she'd seen his face before. *Sean Slagle*. It rang a bell, yet she didn't know why.

Sean shook her hand before they left. "We'll keep you in the loop on the investigation."

"Call me at any time," she said.

"Will do."

Ada had salvaged dinner and ordered everyone to sit at the back table to enjoy the fruits of Rose's labor.

"Y'all should really go home," Rose said, dipping into her Southern accent, which happened when she was upset. She sniffled. "I'm not much for company right now."

"Don't kick us out," Hilary insisted. "We want to be here for you. We want to help you."

Rose dragged herself to the outdoor table and watched as her Salt Sisters doted on her, refilling her wine and giving her overwhelming portions of food. Her friends looked at her nervously but tried to keep their tones bright.

"Tell us more about the Grayson Estate!" Nora begged, her fork filled with greasy bacon and brussels sprouts.

"Who did you buy it from, anyway?" Ada asked.

Rose sniffed, telling them the name the real estate agent had given her—Howard Reynolds. It wasn't a name she knew.

"How did this Howard Reynolds come to own the old Grayson Estate?" Hilary asked.

Rose shook her head.

"He must have bought it. From...?" Robby paused and pressed her lips together.

Rose's heart seized. It wasn't like the name was off-limits. It wasn't like she would fly off the handle the second she heard it.

"He must have bought it from Oren," Rose finished. She chewed a bite of cheese, watching the waves roll against the dock.

"But when would that have happened?" Hilary asked. She looked incredulous, trying to fit together the pieces from Rose's past as though she were a female Sherlock.

"Well, it's been thirty-one years since the fire," Rose said with a shrug. "Sometime between then and now."

"Maybe he wanted to fix it up but decided it was too big of a job," Katrina offered. "Have you looked him up on the internet?"

Rose shook her head and flinched. *What does this have to do with my stolen sculpture?* She wanted to mope in her bedroom alone.

Katrina pulled out her phone and typed out Howard Reynolds, then furrowed her brow.

"It looks like he's a businessman," Katrina said. "Manhattan."

"What kind of business?" Hilary asked.

Rose flared her nostrils.

"Looks like importing and exporting," Katrina said.

"Should we contact him?" Ada suggested. "See why he sold in the first place?"

"The important thing is that it's mine now," Rose said softly. She felt dreamy and sad, and she longed to return to the Grayson Estate and wander through the hallways and think, think, think. For so many months, she'd been dreaming up the very sculpture that had been ripped unceremoniously from her home. *So much wasted time. A piece of my soul was gone.*

Rose pushed herself through the rest of dinner and

took a stack of plates to the kitchen. She slid them into the dishwasher, trying to eavesdrop on the Salt Sisters out on the veranda. It was clear they were talking about her. Did they think she'd lost her mind for buying the Grayson Estate?

She wanted to tell them: *Sometimes, horrible things happen, and it's up to us to make the best of them.*

She wanted to tell them: *We are all the authors of our own destiny.*

But she felt too exhausted.

Rose leaned against the counter and pressed her face into her hands. Exhaustion made her eyes feel heavy and her shoulders droop.

I'm fifty-two years old, she reminded herself, *and for the first time in a long time, I'm afraid.*

She wished she could shake it.

Chapter Seven

June 1993

Rose planned to hitchhike back to the Walden Estate. She felt like a rebel woman, a woman on the brink of the rest of her life, a woman who took risks. After all, she'd come all the way to Nantucket from Mississippi on a wing and a prayer. What was a bit of hitchhiking? It was nothing in comparison.

Rose was at the edge of the Nantucket Historic District with her thumb out. It was nearly ten in the evening, and she felt blurry with happiness and dizzy with freedom. She'd stayed out far longer than she'd planned for, but she hadn't been able to resist window-shopping and people-watching and eating two ice cream cones so that her head felt fuzzy with sugar.

But it was the nineties, not the seventies. Did that mean people didn't hitchhike anymore?

Rose watched with increasing despondency as

tourists passed her by, ignoring her or giving her annoyed looks. Mothers seemed the cruelest of all, frowning when they passed or pressing their foot on the gas, as though Rose's existence on this planet would soon corrupt their children. It was only a matter of time.

This gave Rose pause. What if one of those mothers was friendly with Mrs. Walden? What if they told Mrs. Walden what Rose was up to, and Rose lost her job?

But Rose didn't have much time to consider the what-ifs. Suddenly, a car stopped on the side of the road—a nice car, Italian-made with tinted windows. Rose didn't hesitate. She threw herself into the passenger seat and closed the door behind her.

Immediately, she recognized the man in the driver's seat.

It was Oren Grayson.

It was the man who'd lost his wife, Natalie.

Rose's mouth went dry with panic.

Oren pressed the gas and shifted his massive hands across the steering wheel. He wore a very expensive cologne that Rose wouldn't have been able to name if her life was at stake. But even she—a Southern country girl with two dollars in her pocket—recognized it as remarkable. As something that startled you out of yourself. As something that made you acknowledge the wearer as powerful, mysterious, and handsome.

"Thank you," Rose mustered because she hated how quiet the car was.

She eyed the radio and speaker system, and her fingers itched with urgency. She wanted to turn it on and blare it as loud as it could go.

"Didn't anyone tell you it wasn't safe to hitchhike?"

Oren asked. His gruff voice was like nobody's Rose had ever heard.

I'm so sorry about your wife, Rose wanted to say. And then she remembered that Zachary and Mrs. Walden had hinted that he'd *started the fire himself.*

So had he? Rose inspected his face, his expensive clothes, and his car. He didn't seem like a murderer. Then again, she'd never been around any murderers. What did she know?

"It seems we're staying at the same place," Oren said.

Rose raised her chin. "You're staying with the Waldens?"

"For now."

Rose blinked several times. She'd thought the night of drinks was a one-time thing. Maybe they were perpetually in the lounge with cocktails, listening to records, telling stories, making sure not to say a thing about *Natalie.*

"It's a beautiful place," Rose said.

Oren made a strange noise in his throat. Rose couldn't make sense of it.

For whatever reason—perhaps because she was a masochist or too curious for her own good, she decided to probe. "What do you mean?"

"The Walden Estate isn't so nice." Oren coughed.

"Compared to what?" Rose demanded.

Oren raised his eyebrows, and Rose felt his answer with startling clarity: *not nice compared to the home that just burned down.*

Rose bit her lower lip. Her pulse was frantic. She remembered the way his face had transformed when she'd said, *I'm so sorry for your loss.* Then she realized that

Natalie had sat on the passenger side of this car probably hundreds of times. A chill came over her.

"I'm working for the Waldens," Rose stuttered. "So you can let me know if you need anything." She took a breath. "Okay?"

Oren's eyes flickered over to her as he drove. Rose took a peek at the speedometer and saw they were going twenty-five over the speed limit. It was exhilarating. His wife had just died, but he was still eager to toy with death himself.

Rose thought, *This is the most fascinating man I've ever met in my life.*

They reached the Walden Estate at ten thirty. Oren parked and threw his keys at the on-hand valet and stalked into the night. Rose watched him go, wondering where he was going. The beach for a night swim? He had the kind of wild energy that made it difficult to know where he was off to or if you would ever see him again.

"Rose?"

Rose nearly leaped from her skin. Twisting around, she discovered Mrs. Walden at the edge of the veranda, peering down at her. A long and slender cigarette hung from between two of her fingers. In the moonlight, Mrs. Walden looked especially pale and thin, almost skeletal.

"Rose, will you come up here for a moment?" Mrs. Walden asked without waiting for Rose's hello.

Rose hurried up the steps to the veranda to find Mrs. Walden sprawled out on a bench with her skirts flowing out on either side. Beside her was an empty glass that probably had very recently held one of Mrs. Walden's favorite cocktails. Mrs. Walden's eyes were glazed and half-open.

Rose dropped to her knees beside Mrs. Walden.

Having grown up in a small town in the South, she wasn't unfamiliar with the mannerisms of an alcoholic. But for whatever reason, Rose had assumed that only poor people could be alcoholics. It didn't make sense that a woman with *everything in the world she could ever want* would drink away her blues. What kind of blues had Mrs. Walden ever had? Hadn't her bills always been paid? Weren't her children always fed? Didn't she have the most gorgeous view from a veranda that she never had to leave if she didn't want to?

Rose's head thudded with questions.

"Mrs. Walden? Are you all right?" Rose muttered.

Mrs. Walden's voice was just a rasp. "You need to be careful around him, Rose."

Rose's heart jumped into her throat. She searched the dark beach for some sign of Oren but couldn't find him. Was he listening? Was he somewhere near, laughing about the show Mrs. Walden was putting on? Maybe they would both laugh later and say, *That Rose is sure an idiot, isn't she?*

"You need to listen to me," Mrs. Walden repeated as her eyes closed. "You have to watch it."

Rose retreated inside to find another member of staff who was better equipped to bring Mrs. Walden to her bedroom. Rose wasn't sure if she could have found Mr. and Mrs. Walden's wing again if she searched for it herself. The house was too big, too meandering.

She was exhausted.

Rose hurried back to her bedroom, turned on the lights, and looked at herself in the mirror. She was slightly sunburnt, and her eyes echoed blissful happiness, proof that she was *doing something with her life*. Proof that it was all on her own terms.

But just before she drifted off to sleep, Rose remembered Natalie's image in that newspaper, an obituary that stated her death at the age of twenty-six.

Why is the fire an enormous secret? She marveled in the darkness. *What is everyone hiding?*

Chapter Eight

Present Day

Rose called the client the morning after the robbery to report what had happened. The friend of a friend of Ingrid put herself on video and blinked out expectantly, smiling a California smile and waiting for Rose to put herself on video, too.

"There you are!" the client said brightly. "I was just telling a few friends about the sculpture. I'm floored by the photos you sent. It's truly better than I ever could have imagined."

Rose hesitated. Any initial suspicion that the client had been involved in the robbery dissipated on the spot.

"There's something I have to tell you," Rose murmured, feeling nervous, tugging the ends of her hair.

The client was genuinely distraught. "Did you check your video footage?"

Rose winced and explained there had been a malfunction. *Rose decided she didn't need to know when the malfunction occurred.*

"I'll keep you updated," Rose promised the client before they got off the phone. "I'm sure we'll get to the bottom of it soon."

The client was incredibly displeased. They got off the phone with the air of old ex-friends with nothing else left to say.

Rose poured the rest of the contents of the coffee pot into her mug and left the kitchen to watch seagulls soar over rolling waves. For the better part of the year, she'd woken up and gone immediately to her studio to work on the sculpture. Now, she felt hollow and purposeless.

That was when she remembered the Grayson Estate. *At least I have that.*

Rose went for a ten-mile run through beach trails and lush forests and returned home for a smoothie and a shower. In a lunchbox, she packed a sandwich, some dark chocolate, an apple, and a protein bar, then drove out to the Grayson Estate to find it swarming with construction workers in yellow hats. Rose got out and watched them for a while, noting their easy tenderness as they secured the doorway and the pillars with construction tape.

Charlie was in conversation with a construction worker on the eastern side of the house, his arms spread wide as he discussed the caved-in roof and the yonder gazebo. Rose approached and caught the tail-end of their conversation, including Charlie saying, "As much of the place needs to be accessible so that Rose can start going through stuff. She wants to clear it all out and then refurbish."

"There's a lot of junk in there," the construction worker said.

"There are always treasures in the midst of junk," Charlie said.

Rose appeared beside him and stuck out her hand to shake the construction worker's hand.

His grip was powerful. He grinned and said, "This is some place you got here. It's rare that a burned building like this can take on new life." He traced the rooftop with his gaze again, then asked, "Any idea why the owner abandoned it after the fire?"

Charlie gave Rose a look that meant *I don't have you figured out yet, Rose Carlson. But there's certainly something amiss here.*

He'd remembered Oren.

"The man who owned it when the fire broke out eventually did sell it," Rose said. "But I haven't looked into *why*." She remembered her flippancy toward Howard Reynolds last night over dinner with the Salt Sisters and felt a spike of shame. They'd been trying to help. She'd rejected it.

The construction worker whistled. "It's been weathered over thirty-one years. That's the truth. But I can show you the areas of the house that are safe for you to enter into for now," he said. "Follow me?"

Rose squeezed Charlie's elbow with excitement. Together, the two of them followed the construction worker through the foyer, down the hall, through the kitchen, and back along the edge of the ballroom. As the other construction workers had already warned, the ballroom was a no-go zone, as was much of the second and third floors. But there were numerous hideaways and shadowed rooms that, it seemed, had been completely sealed over the past thirty-one years. White sheets heavy with dust were stretched across sofas and beds and wardrobes; bedrooms were locked, and the wood of the doors warped. Floorboards creaked beneath them as they walked, dipping their heads into musty bathroom walk-in closets.

The library was located at the far end of the first floor and sealed. Miraculously, an iron key hung to the right of the door on a nail and glinted with ancient promise. Rose removed it and slipped it into the library knob, and turned it. She half expected Charlie or the construction worker to tell her not to, to tell her it wasn't safe. But they just watched her.

Like the other sealed rooms, white sheets had been strung over everything of value. None of the windows in this room were broken, as far as she could tell, and the curtains had been drawn long ago, meaning that the books had existed in a sort of tomb for all these years. No sunlight. No rain. Nothing had affected them. Rose pulled aside a sheet to assess an entire row of books—all from the eighteen hundreds and in remarkable condition. She raised her eyebrows.

Oren was always a big reader, she remembered. But she hadn't known he'd had to say goodbye to so many of the books he'd loved.

Why didn't he come back in here to check on them? She wondered.

Unless Oren had returned after the fire. Maybe it had been Oren who'd pulled the white sheets over the bookshelves. Perhaps he'd tried to protect the things he'd left behind.

Rose certainly couldn't imagine Zachary doing something like that. Rather, it was the dark shadow of Oren she felt moving through the old house, his thoughts stirring with anger and sorrow and fear. She felt him here as though he'd only recently been here. As though the years hadn't come between them.

"This is a crazy collection," Charlie said, breaking her reverie. "Some of these books must cost a fortune."

The construction worker remained in the doorway with his arms crossed over his chest. "Whoever sealed this room knew what they were doing."

A heavy moment of silence passed between them. Rose felt Charlie and the construction worker's eyes upon her, sizing her up. She felt their curiosity. *Does she know more than she's letting on?* They seemed to ask.

"I'll start here today," Rose announced. "Thank you again for your help."

Charlie admitted he had to hit the road, and the construction worker was needed back with his crew to secure the ballroom and orchestrate a plan to either bolster the integrity of the old roof or pitch a strategy to rebuild. Rose had told them everything was possible, that money was no object. When she'd said that aloud, she'd winced at herself and thought, *I sound like Mrs. Walden.*

I never wanted to sound like Mrs. Walden.

Rose returned to her car and drove to the nearest store to buy heavy-duty cleaning supplies and face masks to combat the dust. Back in the library, she shoved the dirty sheets into trash bags and cleaned the ancient curtains so she could pull them aside without creating more clouds of dust.

Rose was so consumed by her work that she hardly noticed the passage of time.

Early evening hit and left her ragged with hunger. She stepped out of the library to discover that the construction crew had already left for the day, leaving their tools locked up. Although she still wasn't supposed to, she strode out into the center of the ballroom and spread her arms on either side of her with her chin raised to the ceiling.

It was then she felt an onslaught of nearly forgotten memories.

In her mind's eye, she was twenty-one again. It was time for the party of the season. Mrs. Walden had assured her that she wasn't invited to the party and that it was up to her to remain upstairs with the children, keeping them occupied so they didn't go downstairs to bother the guests. The party was held in the Walden Estate, and all the best, brightest, and most successful Nantucket holidaymakers were invited.

Because Oren was still living with the Waldens at the time, he could not escape. He'd been forced to attend, too.

The fact that Oren had asked Mrs. Walden if the babysitter might join for the ball had caused confusion among the Waldens and their elite friends.

He's grieving, they'd decided. *He doesn't know what he wants.*

But Oren was only six years older than Rose—twenty-seven to her twenty-one. The age gap wasn't ridiculous. It was the monetary gap that made it sensational and so very, very wrong.

"There will be plenty of beautiful women at the party," Mrs. Walden had tried to assure him. *"You don't need to worry yourself with a member of my staff."*

Now, at fifty-two, Rose shook out these memories, fixed her face, and locked up the house for the night.

She'd bought the house to feel a sense of ownership over a past that didn't always make sense to her.

How could she have known what she would discover in that old place?

How could she have known she'd bitten off more than she could chew?

When she got home, she made a grilled cheese sandwich, poured herself a glass of wine, and tended to the messages on her cell—most of which were from the Salt Sisters. They were worried about her after last night.

HILARY: I know you've probably just thrown yourself into a new task to keep yourself occupied.

HILARY: I hope you remember to take care of yourself. You need rest after so much stress.

There was also a voicemail message from Officer Sean Slagle.

"Hi, Rose," he said. "I just wanted to let you know that we've explained your situation to the ferry companies. They've promised to keep an eye out for any oversized packages that weigh as much as your sculpture does."

From the voicemail message came the ruffling of pages and Sean clearing his throat. "I can't imagine we'll let something this massive get away," he said. "Just wanted to let you know I'm in your corner. My mother was, um, an artist. And I know what it might mean to lose something so dear."

Rose's heart twinged with surprise. It was rare to feel such empathy from a man of the law—a man whose job description often entailed "yelling at teenagers" and "giving out tickets for bad drivers." But Rose had long ago realized a fact about humanity, a fact that she continued

68

to return to again and again. People surprised you, regardless of their background, their intelligence, their job description or the way they looked. It was important to remember that you could surprise someone, too, at any time. That was the nature of being alive.

Chapter Nine

July 1993

The stomach bug that attacked Rose on the morning of her day off in week two. It kept her locked in her bedroom, heaving and rolling around on the mattress. She could barely see the children through the window. Together with Miriam, the children walloped and ran around, their arms spread, their legs kicking and dancing. Balls soared through a cerulean sky. But Rose couldn't even join them outside.

Rose was filled with dread and sorrow. It hadn't been the plan to spend her second full day off like this. It was a waste of time.

I'm failing myself, she thought before nearly vomiting again.

Because Rose hadn't been able to pack more than a couple of books, she'd already run out of things to read. She knew there was a library downstairs, an adult one that had nothing to do with the children's book selection upstairs. But she also hadn't specifically asked Mrs.

Walden if she could dip into the library for her personal selection.

Why would it bother her? She wondered now but then remembered that for six full days a week, she was supposed to devote her entire life, mind and heart to the Walden children.

But that evening, through the window, Rose watched as Mr. and Mrs. Walden drove down the driveway and whizzed out of sight. If she wasn't mistaken, Zachary and Oren were in the back seat. It meant they were headed somewhere, probably somewhere exquisite with divine cocktails and food with far more flavor and beauty than anything Rose would ever enjoy.

It meant Rose could tiptoe down the hallway, head downstairs, and select a few books before they returned.

Otherwise, I'll die of boredom, she thought.

The children were dining downstairs with Miriam. As Rose crept, she heard Kate giggling and Evie talking with food in her mouth. Rose's heart swelled with what could only be love for them. *I'm a sap,* she thought now. But she understood that caring for children every day inevitably brought about these sorts of feelings.

Sometimes, Rose wondered if this was proof she wanted children of her own one day. She imagined raising them in a home as immaculate as this: a home with mahogany floors, mid-century paintings, and furniture like *chaise longues.* She imagined her babies taking their first steps next to sculptures Rose had commissioned artists to make for her. She imagined saying things like *Just throw it out. We don't need it.*

Rose reached the library and inhaled the soft and remarkable smell of thousands upon thousands of pages, stories written across centuries. The walls were lined with what had to be two or three thousand books, and the floor was a lush carpeting that she dug her toes into. There were lamps imported from Europe and thickly cushioned chairs and side tables upon which were stacked still more books. Rose wondered if those were specific piles Mrs. Walden had made for herself; maybe she meant to return to them later. It was better not to touch them, just in case she noticed anything amiss.

Mrs. Walden knows the innermost workings of the house. But she can't possibly notice everything, she thought.

Rose felt like a character in a novel. She touched the golden-laced spine of books; she split books open to smell their pages; she took the heaviest one from the far shelf and tried to guess its weight. Twenty pounds? Thirty? Heaving it back on the shelf was difficult; her arms ached.

Rose hadn't heard of most of the novels in the library. Back in Mississippi, she'd read whatever was around, most of which had been romance novels and mysteries. However, the Waldens enjoyed a higher class of literature. Rose wanted to understand what that was.

Suddenly, a sound came from the corner of the library. A creak. Rose whipped around and peered through the shadows to make out a figure in one of the red cushioned chairs. Her heartbeat thwacked in her ears.

Who is it?

Rose hadn't heard anyone come in after her. Did that mean that whoever this was had been here the entire time? Watching her?

A staff member? A friend of the Waldens? Who?

Rose backed toward the doorway with her fingers

spread. She finally mustered the strength to whisper, "Who's there?"

Her eyes remained locked on the dark shadow in the corner. Her brain played still more tricks on her. *Maybe nothing is there at all. Perhaps the illness is poisoning my brain.*

"You don't have to run," the figure stated.

Rose stopped short and gaped at the dark shadow. The voice was Oren's. She would have recognized it anywhere.

Suddenly, she remembered Mrs. Walden's warning to stay away from him. *Is he dangerous? Did he light his own house on fire? But why would someone do that?*

"I thought you went to town with the Waldens," Rose stuttered. She sounded like a child.

Oren stood and walked toward her so that the gray light of the evening filtered through the window and illuminated him. His eyes glinted.

Rose had the strangest sensation that he was a spider, and she'd just walked into his web.

Oren held a book in his right hand. Rose squinted to make out the title: *Jane Eyre.*

"What is that?" Rose asked because the silence was killing her.

Oren raised the book and marked his page. "You don't know it?"

Rose's cheeks flushed. Was she supposed to?

"It's quite old. Written by one of the Brontë sisters," Oren said. His tone was soft and easy. He took a small step and extended his arm to pass the book over. "It was my mother's favorite."

Rose was intrigued. She took the book and studied it,

noting the gold-lined pages, the yellowed edges, and the sturdy spine. "Did this copy belong to your mother?"

"No," Oren said. "I found it here."

Rose raised her chin and felt a surge of fear. Had Oren's mother's copy been lost in the fire along with his wife? *That house on the other side of the forest feels like a black hole,* she thought.

"How many times have you read it?" she asked.

"Two or three," Oren said. "But I'm really surprised you haven't heard of it."

Rose was surprised not to hear a hint of malice in Oren's tone. Mrs. Walden probably would have made her feel really stupid for not having read the book. She might have made a joke about the "failing nature of the American education system in the South." Northern superiority.

"I think I saw another copy," Oren said. "Come on."

Oren led Rose to the opposite side of the library and removed a different version of *Jane Eyre,* one that seemed to have been printed much later than the one in his hands. It seemed less mystical. Rose trusted herself with it more.

"You came here to get a book?" Oren asked.

Rose nodded and pressed the book against her chest. Her stomach continued to roil, but she didn't know if it was due to sickness or nerves.

"I imagined you would leave the house today. Imagined you'd traipse through the island and hitchhike home again," Oren said. "It's your day off, isn't it?"

Rose was surprised that Oren knew anything about her schedule. Perhaps Mrs. Walden had let something slip. Or maybe Mrs. Walden had complained about Rose in some capacity. Rich women always complained about the hired help, Rose assumed.

"I've been sick today," Rose explained.

Oren squinted as though he wanted a better look at her. "You look a little pale."

Rose considered telling him that she'd spent the entire day tossing and turning in bed, sweating and cursing and wishing she was back home in Mississippi. *Not that that would fix anything.*

"Do you want a nightcap?" Oren suggested.

"I beg your pardon?"

Oren's smile lifted. "A little drink before you go back upstairs. What do you say?"

Rose's blood pressure spiked. It had been nearly two weeks since the fire, which meant this man was nearly two weeks into grieving the death of his wife. What could she possibly say to him to help him on this journey?

But she knew she couldn't say no.

There was too much urgency in his eyes.

Besides, she'd had such a nothing, painful, black day. Maybe a nightcap would do her soul some good.

Oren led her up a back staircase to an area of the house she'd never seen before. A statue of a stoic man in a soldier's uniform stood guard at the staircase landing, and a stuffed bird stretched its wings maniacally in mock flight. Rose's hand flinched with the sudden desire to sweep through Oren's.

It felt inevitable that I would come up here with him, she thought. *Even from the first moment I saw him, I sensed something would happen.*

How had she known?

Oren had three rooms to himself: a sitting room, an office with a mahogany desk and impressionist paintings, and a bedroom with a view of the Nantucket Sound. The furnishings were ornate and antique. Rose's first thought was that the children would destroy them if they were here.

Oren entered his study and cracked open a bottle of something thick and brown. Maybe it was whiskey or scotch. Whatever it was, it was nothing Rose's parents had ever enjoyed in the shadows of their reeking living room back in Mississippi. They'd always smoked cigarettes inside. Mrs. Walden smoked, too; Rose had seen her. But they had plenty of maids to clear out the stench.

Oren poured two stiff glasses and gestured for her to sit in the ocher leather chair across from him. She did. He didn't bother with clicking his glass with hers, as though he was beyond those sort of childish celebrations. *He lost his wife. He'll never celebrate again.*

There was a massive golden sculpture of an eagle behind him. It was ostentatious.

Oren caught her looking at it. "It's awful, isn't it?"

Rose sucked in her breath. What did she know about design or artistry? Back home, her parents' idea of decor had been fifteen American flags positioned around the yard and house, stitched upon pillows and bedspreads.

"It's something," she said, hoping she struck the right tone.

Oren got up and looked the golden eagle in the eye with the air of a man preparing to fight it. "The way the Waldens decorate this place boils my blood," he muttered.

Rose snorted with surprise.

"Tell me," he said, gesturing. "Tell me how you would have decorated this room."

Rose tried to envision what she might have added to an empty room. What paint colors might she have chosen? What fabric for the furniture? But being poor meant not knowing the full potential of anything. It meant seeing nothing but boundaries.

Too much silence passed. Rose's cheeks were hot with embarrassment. *He's going to regret inviting me up here. He's going to think I'm stupid.*

But Oren seemed to have forgotten his request. He collapsed back on the sofa and propped his feet up on a table that probably cost more than Rose's parents' entire home. His face was intense, stitched together with wrinkles that aged him far more than his twenty-seven years. Was that because of the fire, too? Rose wanted to reach out and trace the lines.

"I'm tired, Rose," Oren muttered now. His eyes glinted as though tears were about to fall. "I can't go anywhere across the island without hearing how heinous I am." His gaze sharpened. "You don't believe what they're saying, do you?"

Rose was seized with the realization that she had to *carry this man's sorrow for him.* But she was well-practiced in that. She'd done it for her father, for her mother, for her siblings.

"I don't know what they're saying," she lied. "I'm always here at the Walden Estate."

"But when you go into town," he said. "You must hear them talking about how I *burned the place down.* How I killed her."

A knot formed in Rose's throat. She filled her mouth with whiskey and stopped herself from coughing everything up.

"It's ridiculous," Oren muttered, his eyes on the window. "They don't know what they're talking about."

Rose felt meek. She had the sense that Oren would

have asked anyone into his study tonight. He wanted to talk. He didn't want to be alone.

"It's like this," Oren said. "You fall in love, and you do everything you can to stay in love. But sometimes, it slips through your fingers."

Rose had never been in love. She couldn't fully imagine it. It didn't seem to suit the nature of the world in which she'd been raised. *Love in this cruel world? No. Maybe it doesn't exist.*

"Natalie was the kind of woman who always felt misunderstood, no matter what," Oren said. "No matter how hard I tried or how eager I was to please her, she always found fault in me." Oren's voice warbled.

Rose thought, *This man is broken beyond repair.*

"We were doing our best to come back together," Oren whispered. "We went to therapy. We talked and talked till all hours of the night. We tried to make sense of each other. We tried to make sense of our lives." He wrung out his hands. "We were so close, Rose. So close. And that's what I think about the most." Tears drained from his eyes and lined his cheeks. "I can't believe she died in agony like that. I can't believe that's how our marriage had to end."

The room began to spin. Rose was reminded of her illness, of her body and its betrayal. She reached out to him without thinking, and he slid his hand onto hers and squeezed it. A jolt of electricity went through her.

"It's the first time I've been able to talk about this," Oren murmured. "Thank you. Thank you for listening."

Rose said, "Any time. I'm here for you any time."

Her voice was hardly a whisper. Yet what she said seemed like a dense, weighted promise that would drag her under if she wasn't careful.

We have to be there for each other, she thought of humankind. *Oren has no one but me.*

Nothing else happened that first night. It was just two weeks after Natalie left the world behind.

But Rose felt the air between them. It was heavy with expectation. It felt as though their story had already been written. She couldn't wait to turn the page.

Chapter Ten

Present Day

Rose was back in the library at the Grayson Estate. It was early morning, not yet ten, but the construction crew was already hard at work, hammers rocketing. Out the window, she could see a few men in hard hats circling the gazebo, gesturing with their thick arms. One of them had mentioned it was probably best to "rip the gazebo down and start over," but Rose was adamant that they maintain the old structure. "Whatever it takes" was her mantra.

With a cup of coffee in hand, Rose wandered through shelves of books, reading their spines, trying to imagine Oren purchasing them on his adventures around the world—adventures he'd had before he'd met Rose. She stopped short in the B-section, mouth ajar at the sight of *Jane Eyre*. A chill came over her. There was only one copy. Carefully, she pulled it out and held it out in front of her. It felt like something from ancient Rome.

Inside the cover, Oren's mother had written her name.

"It was my mother's favorite," Oren had told her when he'd first recommended the novel that night at the Walden Estate. Still roiling with a stomach bug, Rose had stayed awake all night reading it, trying to uncover the madness behind Oren's eyes. *A man who'd lost everything. A man who'd looked at me as though I could restore his heart.*

Rose's current plan was to go through the first-floor rooms, throwing away anything unrecognizable or worth nothing or too damaged after years of abandonment to be kept. She had trash bags; she had a truck that was ready to be filled. She'd even packed rubber gloves, just in case anything was too gross for hand contact.

Rose got to work that morning in the sitting room nearest the library. Half of the room had been greatly damaged in the fire, and she put on a face mask and gloves and shoved blackened items into bags—pillows and blankets and sofa cushions and pieces of art that no longer revealed anything. Sometimes, she allowed herself to imagine Natalie and Oren sitting here, perhaps reading together quietly or talking about their days. Oren had once maintained that Natalie was the true love of his life. It had always been difficult for Rose not to believe that. The one you lost was always the one you craved.

Rose broke for lunch at one and sat outside with the construction workers, chatting with them about their wives or their children and about previous jobs they'd worked on. It was clear that they weren't accustomed to their clients going out of their way to ask them questions, and they soon loosened up and cracked jokes with Rose.

Rose knew, *They thought I was wealthy and cold like Mrs. Walden always was with staff members.*

But Rose was something else.

"I hate to say this," one of them said, giving her a wry smile, "but there's something in your accent I can't place. You aren't from the East, are you?"

Rose laughed. "It's been a long time since anyone noticed!"

"What is it?" the worker asked, cupping his chin.

"You don't want to wager a guess?" Rose asked.

The construction worker twisted around to address the others. "Who wants to bet on where Rose is really from?"

All hell broke loose after that. Rose ate her sandwich and listened, smiling, as the workers squabbled over where Rose might be from and how much they were willing to bet their guesses. They'd decided that whoever got closest in miles to the original birthplace was the winner, which meant they all got as specific as possible.

"I'm going to guess Nashville, Tennessee," one said.

"I'm going with Atlanta, Georgia," another said.

"Dallas."

"Los Angeles. Look at that skin! She's a California girl."

Nobody said Mississippi, but one of the guys said "New Orleans," and he eventually took the cash prize of sixty-two dollars. He grinned sheepishly, showing his dimples.

"How did you know she was from the Deep South?" one of them asked him.

"I didn't," he said. "But I always wanted to go to New Orleans. I figured I'd take my chance." He blinked at Rose. "Have you been to New Orleans?"

Rose hesitated. "I always wanted to go."

"It's so close to where you grew up!" he said.

Rose remembered the dimly lit living room, her brothers and sisters screaming and tearing everything apart, her mother's tired eyes, and her father's cruelty.

"Traveling wasn't really on my radar until I left home," Rose said.

"But you're well-traveled now," the worker said. It was almost like an accusation.

"Yes. I suppose so." Rose placed her half-eaten sandwich back in its foil. "I guess that means I'd better get down to New Orleans."

"It's waiting for you," the man said.

Rose returned to her work with even more rigor—and an even deeper comprehension of the immensity of her task. She threw things away tirelessly, created piles of items that seemed worth something, and hunted for Oren in the small details, in the stopwatch on a dresser, in a painting that she thought might be of his mother when she was a teenager. She found an old note from Zachary to Oren, in which Zachary said he'd meet him at the horse barn at seven o'clock. Zachary called him "a rascal" in the note.

It was the first time Rose had thought of Zachary in a while. Where did he live now?

Rose pulled up Zachary's name online and read a brief article about Zachary's recent sale of a company for twenty-two million dollars. The featured photograph showed him as a typical sixty-something-year-old super-elite Manhattan resident. He was on his fourth wife.

Rose noted that he still had that bright smile. It helped him get away with just about everything.

The rest of that day and the two after that were the

same. Rose worked and cleaned and piled, making sense of a space that she'd never dreamed would be hers. She ate with the construction workers and got to know them better, teasing them and baking their favorite treats.

All the while, Sean Slagle updated her on the search for her stone sculpture. "We haven't found it yet," he admitted.

It was the end of the third day that Rose discovered Natalie's room.

Rose was on the second floor of the Grayson Estate, wearing a ratty white T-shirt and a pair of jeans with holes in the knees. Outside was stormy, gray clouds stirring and frothing as though they were in a blender. Rose listened to the construction workers arguing about something in the ballroom—something about whether or not the roof would really hold. She winced and said a brief prayer. *Please save that gorgeous ceiling.*

The room was at the opposite end of the house from where the fire had broken out and had been sealed, most of it covered with plastic and white sheets, its curtains closed against the sun. Rose entered, thinking it was just another guest bedroom at first. *Another bedroom for the future bed and breakfast.*

Rose pulled a thick plastic sheet off a piece of art on the wall. Her heart dropped into her stomach.

Natalie.

Here was a glossy portrait of Oren's first wife, dressed in her wedding gown. She was probably twenty or twenty-one in the painting, so terribly delicate and young, her pretty hands crossed on her lap, her blue eyes crystalline. Rose's eyes filled with tears. *The woman who died in the fire. The woman who lost her life in this very home.*

Oren's great love.

Rose continued to remove plastic sheets and bedsheets to reveal a quaint little room with a secretary desk, a Turkish rug, and maybe two hundred books— Rose's favorite books. Inside the desk were fountain pens and photographs from Rose's life before Oren, photographs that weren't pressed into any books and hung loosely in drawers. The photos showed Natalie as a beautiful and pale little thing, her arms around her girlfriends, her eyes alight. Based on her clothes, Rose guessed that Natalie hadn't come from money, either. She didn't know why that surprised her so much. She'd initially thought Natalie came from Oren's world, that they'd met because they were blessed with families with deep pockets. But it looked like Oren had scooped Natalie out of nowhere.

She's like me, Rose thought.

She cursed herself for never asking Oren where he'd met Natalie. She'd thought it better to avoid the topic at all costs.

Here I am, faced with the mystery of Natalie—the woman my husband could never get over.

Tucked away in the bottom drawer of the secretary's desk was Natalie's diary.

It was the size of Rose's hand. No lines. Soft pages. Her tight, feminine handwriting.

Rose's heart thudded. She couldn't believe this. Then again, wasn't something like this part of the reason she'd wanted to buy the house in the first place? She'd wanted to dig into the undiscovered pieces of a past she couldn't fully comprehend. She'd wanted to make sense of her life —and therefore Natalie's life, cut too short?

Rose flipped to the last entry to find the date: June 16, 1993.

Tears filled Rose's eyes. She stared at the date—the date of the fire—and felt as though she floated. She imagined herself at twenty-one on the opposite side of the forest, watching the smoke and the helicopter. At that very moment, a young and beautiful woman had been here. At that very moment, she'd been dying. Nobody had been able to save her.

Rose filled her lungs and read:

June 16, 1993

Sometimes I think back to my first days with Oren. I remember the way he held me, the way he kissed me, the way he promised me everything. The entire world and everything I wanted inside of it. His entire heart.

I never could have imagined this.

I live in terror of him.

It's impossible to say what he'll be like when he wakes up in the morning. On the rare mornings we wake up in the same bed, I peek over and watch his face, watch his mood come over him. If his eyes glint evilly, I make myself scarce.

If I don't run away from him if I don't give him space? There's no telling what he'll do. The bruises up and down my right arm are proof of that.

I don't know if I'll make it out alive.

Rose snapped the book closed, her blood pressure skyrocketing, her tongue scratchy. Slowly, she walked to the window and peered out at the construction workers, lined up in raincoats and smoking cigarettes. She breathed a sigh of relief. *I'm in the year 2024,* she reminded herself. *Natalie has been gone for thirty-one years. I haven't seen Oren in what feels like forever.*

But Natalie's words felt so prescient, so terrifying. They rattled through Rose's mind.

Rose protected the diary with a plastic bag and left the Grayson Estate a few minutes later. Although she initially planned to drive straight to Hilary's for a Salt Sisters dinner, she cut early and went into town, parking outside the police station. It was nearly five thirty. Sean Slagle had said he was in every day till seven if something didn't take him out of the office.

Rose approached the front desk at the police station with the plastic-wrapped diary pressed against her stomach. She felt like a girl in the principal's office. She wondered if anyone ever felt fully grown up or if it was always just an act.

"Hi! Is Officer Slagle still here?" she asked.

"Let me check," the receptionist said. She dialed into his office, and the phone rang and rang and rang.

Rose felt despondent. She wasn't sure she could wait another day before sharing what she'd found. *It's taken thirty-one years for anyone to dig deeper into this. Why?*

"He's not there," the receptionist said. "But I can leave a note and have him call you back tomorrow?"

"I'll be back tomorrow," Rose said. "Thank you."

Rose left the office and wandered through downtown with her heart in her throat, thinking back to those long-lost days when she'd been a nobody-babysitter for the Waldens; when she'd hardly had a few pennies to rub together and had spent her days off stretched out on public beaches, eavesdropping on tourists. Everything had sizzled with magic. She'd been so curious about this world that she hadn't understood.

The diner where she'd gone on her first day off in 1993 was still open all these years later. Rose didn't go often; it was out of her way, and she didn't eat as many greasy meals as she had at twenty-one. But sometimes she dipped in to have a slice of pie and chat with the servers, some of whom had worked there thirty-one years ago, too. It felt as though they'd gone through time together.

Rose grabbed her favorite booth and placed Natalie's diary on the seat beside her. A server by the name of Brenda approached to say, "Rosie, darling! How long has it been?"

Rose smiled and asked Brenda about her grandchildren and the garden that remained her pride and joy. Brenda was frustrated about her grandson. She just couldn't get him excited about mathematics. "Computers are everything these days. If he wants a job, he needs to learn how all that works!"

"He's still young," Rose assured her. "Little boys like running around and getting into scrapes."

"I know. There's still time." But Brenda looked worried. "Do you want your usual?"

"Actually, I'll have a burger today," Rose said, surprising herself. She didn't feel up for the Salt Sisters dinner. She knew it would be obvious how upset she was about Natalie's diary, and she didn't want to field questions from Hilary. Not today.

"Fries? Onion rings?"

"Can I get a mix of both?"

Brenda winked. "Anything for our girl."

That was when the door sprang open, bell jangling. Brenda and Rose turned to watch as a familiar man dressed in uniform appeared, adjusting his hat.

It was Sean.

Chapter Eleven

"I've been looking all over for you!" Rose said as Sean approached her table, his smile curious and handsome, so handsome that it tugged at something Rose thought was dormant inside her.

It occurred to Rose that she'd thought of Sean quite often over the past few days. Due to the impending investigation, he'd been a consistent name on her cell phone screen. She'd listened to his voicemail messages, grateful for his tireless efforts. *Someone who is honest and respectable in this crazy world.*

Brenda arched a perfectly drawn eyebrow at both of them and tapped her notepad with her pencil. "What can I do for you, Sean?"

"I'll have whatever she's having," Sean said.

"Burger and fries and onion rings?"

"Apparently so," Sean said, his smile widening. "So much for my diet."

Rose laughed. "It's been a crazy day. I needed to coat my stomach with grease."

"I've had that kind of day, too," Sean said. He

removed his hat to show puffs of strange-looking curls that he attempted to flatten with his hand. "I wish I could share more news about your sculpture."

Rose shook her head, surprised that she'd spent so much time not thinking about the robbery at all. Sean remained standing at her table, glancing around. Did he want to sit with her? Or had he come here for a bit of privacy and deep thought, as she had?

"You can sit down if you want," Rose stuttered.

"I don't want to interrupt."

"I told you already," Rose said. "I've been looking for you. It's fate that you came in here."

Sean hesitated before dropping into the opposite side of the booth. Rose touched the plastic-wrapped diary with the tips of her fingers and told herself not to spring too much on him at once. He'd had a hard day.

Soon after, Brenda brought them two glasses of Diet Coke. She hadn't asked. She knew what they liked.

"How often do you come here?" Sean asked.

"I haven't been in a few months," Rose admitted. "But I came here my first week in Nantucket thirty-one years ago. It's been a favorite since then."

It was where she'd first read Natalie's obituary. It was where she'd learned that so much of the island assumed Oren had been the one to start the fire—and kill Natalie.

I shoved that into the back recesses of my mind for years, Rose thought. *I need answers now.*

"Do you come often?" Rose asked because she was too frightened to dive immediately into the darkness.

"Once or twice a week. They take care of me here."

Rose smiled and glanced at his ring finger to find it empty. She wasn't sure why she'd assumed he was single. He was probably just a little bit older than she was.

Maybe he'd been married before. Perhaps he had grown children.

It was easy to assume many things about a person. Those assumptions were often never correct.

Sean sipped his Diet Coke and held her gaze for a steady moment. Rose's heart thumped.

"Why were you looking for me?" he asked.

Rose reached for the diary and placed it on the table between them. Her vision blurred with tears, but she blinked them away quickly, cursing herself for showing her hand.

"You know I bought the old Grayson Estate," she said, fingers splayed over the diary.

Sean nodded and remained quiet. His eyes were impossible to read. Maybe that was what made him a good cop.

"I've been going through everything," she said. "Throwing things out. Seeing what might be of value. I want to refurbish it and open a hotel or bed-and-breakfast. Something like that."

"You've never been inside?" Sean asked.

Rose shook her head, although she was surprised at the question. *What does Sean know about me?* Then again, Sean hung out here at the diner. Sean was a resident of Nantucket. It meant he was privy to all sorts of gossip.

I wonder what the island says about me buying that old place. The judgment never ends.

"A lot of the house was sealed off like a tomb," Rose said. "It means a lot of the books and art were saved. But today, I discovered a room on the second floor that seems to have belonged to Natalie." Rose's voice warbled when she said Oren's first wife's name. She couldn't remember the last time she'd said the name aloud. Natalie had always existed as a character in her mind. The diary made her real.

Rose paused for a beat to make sure Sean knew who Natalie was. He didn't ask any questions.

"This is her diary," Rose said, pressing the little book across the table. "I read the last entry and knew I needed to talk to someone immediately."

Rose filled her mouth with Diet Coke and watched Sean read Natalie's neat and beautiful handwriting. She half expected his jaw to hang open with surprise. But Sean was a professional. He kept his face stoic.

"It forced me to remember that first summer I was here," Rose said when Sean raised his head. "Everyone was so sure that Oren started the fire. That he was the one who *killed* Natalie. The gossip was everywhere. If you were here, you remember it."

Rose lowered her voice. Across the restaurant, Brenda's eyes continued to flit over, taking stock of her, listening. Rose knew that whatever she said now would be used as gossip for later. But right now, she didn't care. People could say whatever they wanted about her, about her life.

"But Oren spent the summer at the Walden Estate in 1993," Rose continued. "I don't remember any kind of investigation being conducted. I can't understand why. Why didn't the cops go through the Grayson Estate? Why didn't they look through Natalie's things? Why didn't they arrest him or question him?"

Rose felt breathless. "If they'd read that entry, there would have been a trial. Right? I mean, he *hurt* her. She was terrified of him. Isn't that reason enough for a trial?"

Rose was on the edge of her seat, hands spread flat across the diner table. Sean remained quiet. Contemplative. For a moment, Rose was terrified that she hadn't said anything aloud. That her thoughts were turning tight circles, but she hadn't opened her mouth at all.

Brenda appeared with their burgers, fries, and greasy onion rings. Her voice was overly bright, proof that she wanted to linger and listen to their conversation.

"It looks great, Brenda," Rose said. She felt on the brink of tears.

Justice for Natalie! I want justice for all the women in Oren's life!

Brenda disappeared into the kitchen. Sean folded his hands in front of him. He seemed not to notice the burger, the melting cheese, or the bright tomato planted on top. He looked captivated by Rose.

And then he said something that startled Rose out of her skin.

"You don't remember me, do you?"

How was it possible that Rose had forgotten?

Chapter Twelve

July 1993

It was three days after Rose's nightcap with Oren in
his private room. She hadn't seen him since and had
all but convinced herself it hadn't happened at all.
The only proof was her copy of *Jane Eyre,* which she'd
torn through and begun again. She was so hungry to talk
to Oren about it. She ached for her next day off, hoping
she could swing into his private quarters and talk his ear
off about Mr. Rochester and Jane.

Rose dug through the chaos of a typical day at the
Walden Estate. Hogarth was midway through his tennis
lesson, and Kate was studying French, which meant Rose
had two hours with Hamilton and Evie, making up games
and running along the beach. Clouds frothed in the
distance, threatening rain. Rose hated rainy days when
she was babysitting. It meant being cooped up inside,
where the children's voices were so much louder. Rose
was apt to have a headache within the hour.

Once, Rose had let the children play outside in the

rain. They'd gotten drenched and laughed themselves silly—letting out that boundless childish energy that was required if they were going to get to bed on time and sleep through the night. But Mrs. Walden had seen them soaking wet and launched into a diatribe about her children's health and safety. When she'd left, Rose had rolled her eyes into the back of her head. It was all about appearances with her.

Evie took a stick and drew a smiley face in the sand. Hamilton took that opportunity to run through it, tearing it apart with his toes. Evie burst into tears and ran to Rose, burrowing her face in her thighs. Rose snorted and looked at Hamilton.

"Are you going to apologize to your sister?"

Hamilton scampered off toward the waves, calling out, "No."

Rose strung her fingers through Evie's hair. "He's just a mean big brother," she explained.

Evie hiccuped and nodded. She was too sad to speak.

But Rose knew the smiley face would be forgotten in just a few minutes.

"Let's draw something else," Rose said, eager to get Evie's mind elsewhere. She picked up a stick. "What would you like?"

"An elephant," Evie said.

Rose brought an image of an elephant to her mind's eye and began to sketch. She was nervous. It had been a little while since she'd tried to draw something.

Voices came from up the walkway. Evie perked up, hopeful that it was her mother coming to spend time with her. That happened so rarely, but Evie never lost hope.

Instead, three cops appeared at the far end of the walkway. Rose stopped sketching to watch. Two of the cops were in their forties or fifties with big bellies, but one was in his twenties, maybe just a little older than Rose, with dirty blond hair that spilled out of his cop hat.

One of them clambered up the steps to the back porch and knocked on the door. They'd probably already knocked on the front door but had no answer. Where was Miriam?

That was when the younger one spotted Rose. In a flash, they approached, bumbling down the walkway, their eyes on Rose. They looked at her as though she had all the answers to their questions. Rose's throat filled with dread.

Evie hurried up to say hello. "What are you doing here?" she demanded brightly.

The cops stopped and smiled down at her. They were Nantucket cops, which meant they weren't accustomed to hard crime and spent much of their days saying hello to tourists and high-fiving children.

The blond cop watched Rose ponderously.

"We're just here to ask some questions," one of the older cops said. He raised his chin to look Rose in the eye. "Do you know where we can find Mr. or Mrs. Walden?"

"They're not home right now," Rose said. They hadn't told her where they were off to, but they never told her that kind of thing.

"Any idea of when they'll be back?"

"Probably late," Rose said.

"What about Oren Grayson or Zachary Grayson?" the younger blond cop asked. "Are they around?"

Rose raised her eyebrows. *Does this have something to do with the fire?* Rose suddenly felt protective over Oren, as though it was up to her to stand between him and the long arm of the law. *He didn't do anything wrong. He loved Natalie. His heart is broken.*

"No," Rose said, her tone dark. "What is this regarding?"

"We just want to ask the Graysons about the fire from the sixteenth of June," an older cop said. "Have they mentioned anything to you about it?"

"No. I'm just a babysitter," Rose said.

"But working here means you probably overhear things," the blond cop suggested.

"I'm always with the kids," Rose insisted. "We talk about dinosaurs and math problems. That's about it."

The cops exchanged glances. One of the older ones riffled through his pocket to remove a business card, which he passed over. "That has my private number on it," he explained. "Call that when and if you hear anything of value."

Rose took the business card and considered throwing it on the ground.

"Remember that these people don't care about you," he said. "You're their employee. You're replaceable. If they've committed a crime, it means they're dangerous. You don't want anything to do with that."

Rose sniffed and stuffed the business card into the pocket of her sweatshirt. She imagined Oren upstairs, watching over her. She imagined him thinking, *She's protecting me. She's good for me.*

Later that night, Rose crept around downstairs, attempting to eavesdrop on the Waldens or the Graysons. She wanted to know what the cops knew.

The only thing she caught that night was Mrs. Walden saying, "I just keep telling him to get a better lawyer."

Does he really need a better lawyer? He didn't do it!
Rose thought.

That was when the door between the living room and her hiding place burst open, and Rose had to scramble to get back upstairs. It was a good thing she did. Evie was already stationed outside her door, wanting to sleep in her bed. Rose scooped her up and brought her there, grateful for the company.

* * *

Rose's third week of work meant her third day off. Now, the difference was that she'd been paid and had money to burn. This was a first in her life. She decided to hitch a ride with Baxter downtown and spend the day doing whatever she wanted.

Baxter was just as chipper as ever, chatting happily as they cut across the island.

Rose got up the nerve to ask Baxter about Oren and the investigation.

"What do I think?" Baxter repeated. "About if he did it or not?"

Rose nodded.

"I think it doesn't matter what happened," Baxter said. "It never does with these rich folks. They can do whatever they want and get away with it."

Rose thought back to a kid she'd gone to high school with. He'd stolen a candy bar from a gas station and spent the next eight months in juvenile detention. It was clear that if Hogarth or Hamilton or Kate or Evie ever stole a candy bar, they'd get away with it.

The world was upside down.

Baxter dropped Rose off downtown, and Rose spent

the next few hours shopping, trying on clothes, buying dresses and skirts, and imagining herself in Oren's private room, showing off what she'd gotten. She couldn't help but daydream about him. He'd opened up a fantasy world in her mind, one she'd never known she could build. She'd known leaving Mississippi would change everything. But this was bigger than she ever could have imagined.

Rose worked up an appetite and went to the diner for a grilled cheese, reading *Jane Eyre* between bites. After that, she left and swept down the beach, her eyes on the cirrus clouds. The Nantucket Sound sparkled.

Suddenly, she spotted a familiar face.

Standing along the boardwalk in his police clothes was the handsome blond officer who'd come to the Walden Estate the other day. His jaw was sharp and firm, his blue eyes catching the light of the water. He held her eye contact for a few seconds before striding toward her with his hand raised.

Rose's heartbeat intensified. She couldn't run away from him, not now that he'd seen her and was beckoning for her. Would he chase her if she walked away? Did that qualify as breaking the law?

Rose approached him with clammy hands.

"Good afternoon," he said.

"Hi."

"Enjoying your day?"

Rose raised her shoulders and decided to probe a little bit. If they were on the verge of arresting Oren, maybe she could warn him and get him out of here. Maybe he'd even take her with him wherever it was he went.

"How is your investigation going?" Rose asked, her voice light and breezy.

Katie Winters

The officer touched his belt and gave her a look that meant *you know I can't tell you that.*

"We're still looking into everything," the officer said. "I hope we didn't frighten you the other day."

"I'm not easily frightened."

"I guess not." The officer pressed his lips together. "What is that accent?"

"Mississippi."

"You're a long way from home," the officer said. "How did the Waldens find you?"

"I answered an ad in the paper," she said.

The officer cocked his head. "How is the gig? Are the Waldens treating you all right?"

Rose knew he was prying for the sake of his investigation, but she felt no real allegiance to Mr. and Mrs. Walden. "They're fine. They treat me like an employee. It's enough for me. For now." She swallowed, then added, "I just wanted to leave Mississippi."

Why did I tell him that? Why do I want him to know anything about me?

"What about Oren Grayson?" the cop asked.

Rose sniffed. "What about him?"

"I mean, what does he seem like? How does he treat you?"

"He's really kind," Rose answered. "More human than the Waldens."

The cop looked taken aback.

Rose felt her lips break into a smile. She hadn't expected that. "You can't really think Oren killed his wife. That's just island gossip. You shouldn't give in to that."

"Like I said, we're just investigating right now."

"I think you're wasting your time," Rose said. "The

fire was a tragic accident. You're dragging an innocent man's name through the mud."

"What makes you so sure he's innocent?" the cop asked.

They held each other's gaze for a moment. Rose felt as though they played a mental game of chicken. Who would give in first?

"Anyway, I can't talk about this," the cop said, his tone lighter.

"I imagine you can't."

The cop laughed. He suddenly looked nervous. But even Rose couldn't have guessed what he said next.

"What are you doing this weekend?"

Rose bit her lip. It had been a long time since she'd considered the weekend or her potential plans for it.

"I have to work," she said.

"Yeah, but what about after the kids go to bed?" the cop pressed. "There's a beach party. Loads of islanders will be there." He paused, then added, "I'm sure I could get you a different job on the island, too. Something that didn't require you to live with a borderline-insane and very rich family and a potential murderer."

Rose's chest spiked with heat. *He's not a murderer.*

"I have to work all weekend," Rose said. "This is my only day off."

"More reason for me to find you a different job."

But Rose didn't want to be indebted to some cop.

Even more than that, Rose didn't want to leave Oren behind. She couldn't fathom why.

"I'm all right, thanks," Rose said. "But enjoy the party."

Rose ducked around the cop, but the cop kept up with her, maintaining eye contact.

"I'm Sean, by the way," he said. His eyes were like a puppy dog's. "Officer Sean Slagle."

"Hi, Sean. I'm Rose Carlson," she said, feeling light and snappy and alive. "Don't you have some crimes to stop somewhere? Some tickets to write?"

Sean's eyes danced as though he wasn't accustomed to meeting anyone like Rose. "You'll let me know if Oren says anything?"

"I'll let you know if the nicest man I've ever met insinuates that he murdered the love of his life," Rose shot back sarcastically. "Thanks for all your hard work, Officer. Have a great day."

With that, Rose scampered down the beach, sand flying out behind her.

She could feel Officer Sean Slagle watching her every move.

Chapter Thirteen

Present Day

It was remarkable how the memories returned—first slowly and then all at once, like a deluge after a leak in the ceiling. Rose sat at the diner in front of her burgers, fries, and onion rings, remembering how Sean all those years ago asked her to the party that weekend and how her heart had already been latched to Oren's.

Sean raised his eyebrows and took a bite of his onion ring. "This is the kind of thing I would have loved to have back in '93," he said, gesturing toward the diary. "Like you said, everyone was sure Oren had set the fire himself. That he'd done it to kill her, but we could never get any traction on the case."

Rose picked up her burger and took a small bite. Melted cheese and roasted onions took her to another dimension of flavor. She had to stop herself from moaning. *I don't know this guy,* she reminded herself. *But we have a pretty strange history. And now we're here. Together.*

Is that why he was so eager to find my sculpture?

"You couldn't get a warrant to search the house?" Rose asked.

"It was deemed an accident, and then it was sealed up," Sean said. "I think some money changed hands to make sure we couldn't search the place. I was twenty-four at the time. New on the force. I didn't have a lot of leeway, and they definitely weren't telling me everything that went on."

Rose remembered how big-eyed Sean had looked that day on the boardwalk after he'd asked her out. He'd been so hungry to prove himself as an officer. He'd been so sure that Rose knew something.

Now, Sean wiped his hands on his napkin. "He never said anything about the fire or Natalie?"

Rose traced through the memories readily available to her, closing her eyes. Pain rocketed through her.

"He stopped wanting to talk about her and the fire at all," she remembered. "He wanted to bury it all in the past."

"So he could start over with you," Sean said. His tone was dark.

Rose wondered if he was jealous. But how could he be? This was thirty-one years ago. So deep in the past that it was sepia in her mind.

Sean looked incredulous. "You're saying much of the house is still intact?"

"There could be a few more diaries where this came from," Rose affirmed. "But is a diary like this proof of anything?"

"It could be enough to get the case going again," Sean said.

Rose's heart pumped. "I want to be clear. I didn't bring this to you to get revenge."

Sean continued to look at her.

"I haven't seen him in years," Rose said. "He's nothing to me anymore. Just a ghost."

"I understand."

Rose closed her eyes as her thoughts thundered. "I was so naive back then. I'd just left my hometown. I didn't know anything about the world. And I wanted to believe everything he said. I wanted so desperately to fall in love."

Sean was quiet for a little while. Empathy echoed from his eyes.

"If he really did something to Natalie," Rose said, "then I want him to pay for it. I want everyone to know what he did. I don't care if it turns my name to mud in the process."

Sean's eyes hardened. "Why would it turn your name to mud?" he asked. "Like you said, he hasn't been in your life in years. You've built your life from the ground up."

Rose chuckled sadly, remembering those loose and chaotic years after he'd thrown her to her knees like a piece of trash.

Sean raised another onion ring. His eyes shone. "Let's put this guy behind bars."

Rose let out a wild laugh, one that captured the attention of every eye in the diner.

"I'm in," she said, feeling like a woman in a crime novel. "I hope I'm not thirty-one years too late?"

* * *

Rose missed the Salt Sisters' dinner but managed to swing by for post-dinner cocktails. A few Salt Sisters still remained in the glowing orange light of Hilary's veranda, including Robby and Stella and Ada and Katrina. Hilary urged her to sit and tell them "all about the Grayson Estate."

Rose didn't wait long to tell them everything about the diary. She'd taken pictures of the final entry and of a few choice pages throughout the latter part of 1992 and early part of 1993 before Natalie's death.

Hilary read a passage from December 1992 out loud.

"That's the thing about marrying a wealthy man," Hilary began, putting on a slightly different voice. It was proof Hilary came from the acting business. "Everything is a monetary exchange to them. Everything is about goods and services. I didn't understand it when I first met Oren. He doted on me hand and foot. He made me feel like a queen. I still remember that first morning I woke up at his place in Nantucket, with the sunshine spilling through the window and across the sheets. I thought, *This is the happiest I've ever been. He will take care of me.* But he knew how little money I had in the bank. He knew he could butter me up and reel me in.

"Just once did his brother Zachery warn me. It was Christmastime several years ago, and Zachary had drunk his way through a couple of bottles of one-thousand-dollar wine. He tried to put his arm around me, but I swatted him off. He said, *'If you ever do that to Oren, he'll hit you back much harder.'* That surprised me! I went upstairs to cry and cry. But I told myself Zachary was just teasing me. How silly I was not to hear him."

The Salt Sisters sat in steady silence, listening to the

ocean's roar as the sun, like a big egg yolk, dropped into the water.

Rose felt Hilary's heavy gaze but struggled to look at it. She knew what they were all thinking before they asked.

"Rose, did he...?" Stella whispered.

The words hung in the air. *Did he ever beat me?*

Rose remembered his rage. The terror that hung in her chest like a tumor. She realized that ever since she'd found the diary, she'd begun to imagine herself as Oren's wife in that mansion, burning and screaming and falling to her knees. Because Rose had been Oren's wife, too, it wasn't hard to imagine.

Too much time had passed. Rose hadn't answered yet. It felt too complicated.

Hilary took a breath. Rose flinched and looked at her.

"Where in the house did she die?" Hilary asked.

"They always said it was in the kitchen," Rose said.

"And have you been in the kitchen?" Stella asked.

Rose swallowed. "Not yet."

The kitchen needed far more refurbishment than the rest of the house. It was charred, and its windows were broken. A few construction workers suggested that a family of rats and squirrels had taken refuge there. Rose was relieved that she couldn't go in there. She felt sure that the nightmare of Natalie's final moments remained.

"It's insane to me that these secrets were locked inside that house for the past thirty-one years," Ada said.

"Sean said it was difficult to keep the case going. He thinks money changed hands," Rose said. "Back then, Sean begged me for information. He was sure that Oren had let something slip. I'm sure he saw me, a pretty and naive twenty-one-year-old girl, in that dark Walden

Estate and knew that Oren was after me. But Oren already had me wrapped around his finger."

Hilary touched Rose's shoulder tenderly. "You were married to him much longer than Natalie was."

Rose's adrenaline spiked. *How was that possible?*

"He never said anything about doing this?" Stella asked. "He never let anything slip?"

"Never." Rose's heart pumped.

She considered telling the girls that she wasn't trying to put this on Oren for reasons of jealousy or revenge.

"Natalie has never been far from my mind," Rose said instead, her voice wavering. "I feel closer to her than ever. I think I feel I owe her something, especially now. Maybe that's why I wanted to buy the old house. I wanted to put the pieces together. I wanted to make sense of my life, as well as hers."

Rose's eyes filled with tears.

I'm so grateful he let me live, she thought.

She hadn't considered that yet.

"I could never figure Oren out," Rose whispered. "Not for one second of our romance. Not for one second of our marriage. Sometimes, I wonder if the devastation of our marriage is the reason I haven't been able to find love again. Sometimes, I wonder if Oren ruined me."

The other Salt Sisters exchanged glances. Rose could see it in their eyes. *They'd wondered the same thing.*

They urged her to say if she needed help.

But what could Rose do but continue to go through Natalie's things? What could she do but continue to fall down the rabbit hole of her ex-husband's first wife's life?

Chapter Fourteen

August 1993

Rose had begun to break the rules.

She was getting rash about it, breaking past Mrs. Walden's boundaries and rules in the style of a woman with nothing to lose. The reality, of course, was that she had *everything to lose*. But she'd once heard that life began at the edge of her comfort zone. Wasn't that why she'd left Mississippi in the first place? Wasn't that why she'd come all the way here?

After the children went to bed most nights of the week, she changed her clothes, put on lipstick, and tiptoed through the massive house to find Oren in his quarters with a bottle of whiskey and plenty to say. It was these evenings that enlivened her. Oren seemed to have ideas about everything: novels and movies and travel and politics. Rose had never met anyone like him before. She found herself obsessing over what he'd told her the night before, so much so that she was often distracted from her duties with the children. She paid for this a few times when one of the boys got hurt when she should have been watching or when Evie threw a rock at Kate after Kate teased her too much. Rose always hopped to it, remembering herself and what she'd come there to do. She had to protect the children. She had to remain awake, even if she was borderline obsessed with Oren and wanted to think about nothing else.

A private part of her mind said, *Soon, I won't have to worry about babysitting. I'll be someone's bride.*

Rose knew it wasn't right. She knew that Oren had just lost his wife and that he was still grieving. A part of her was terrified that he would shake himself free of the summer, move to the city and find a bride there, somebody who better suited him. Somebody who actually knew more about literature, movies, and psychology. But for whatever reason, he remained at the Walden Estate, waiting for something. Sometimes, Rose liked to guess that he stayed there for her.

That August night, a storm rolled over the island and slashed lightning bolts through the sky. Rose hovered at the window of Oren's study with a glass of whiskey in her hand. Oren was playing Prince on vinyl, and he was more animated than she'd seen him, dancing around. Twice, he touched her on the shoulder and sang, his eyes on hers. A shiver ran down her spine.

Tonight was important for two reasons.

One, this was the last time Oren ever spoke about Natalie.

Two, this was the first night Oren and Rose kissed.

Natalie came up because of Prince.

Oren said, "Natalie always hated this song."

And Rose said, "How could she? It's so good!"

Oren's lips twisted into a smile. "I knew you had a more advanced mind when it comes to music."

Rose beamed. She tried to parse through her memories for proof of that, something she'd said or done that indicated she knew more about music than others. But the fact that Oren said it aloud had to be enough.

"I have to wonder sometimes," Oren said. "Would Natalie and I have gotten divorced if she was still here?"

Rose kept a soft smile on her lips. She wanted to consider that Oren could never have loved Natalie the way he was falling in love with Rose. She had to believe it.

Oren stopped dancing and leaned against his desk. Behind him, lightning veined the night sky. Rose swayed in time to the music, wanting him to think she was beautiful and was always *in the moment.*

"Sometimes I wonder if she ever really loved me," Oren said.

Rose stopped her swaying. Her heart felt bruised from all this Natalie talk. *What about me?* She wanted to yell. But that was childish. It would prove to him that she wasn't ready for him.

"Why do you think that?" Rose breathed.

Oren cocked his head. "Natalie was engaged when I met her."

This was news to Rose. She swallowed, hating the image of Oren sweeping Natalie off her feet—and away from her fiancé. It wasn't so difficult to see how it had happened. Oren was everything a man should be—handsome, powerful, and intelligent. He had a mastery of language unmatched in all of Mississippi or the rest of the world, as far as Rose was concerned.

"She loved him?" Rose asked meekly because she couldn't think of anything else to say.

Oren touched his ear. "She brought him up during arguments," he said darkly. "She always said he would have done *this* or *that* better, that he would never have done *this or that* to her."

"What kinds of things?" Rose asked, frustrated with Oren's vagueness.

"It doesn't matter." Oren hung his head. "Maybe she never should have left him. Maybe everything would have been better."

Rose took a hesitant step toward him and touched his shoulder. She had no idea what to say. *He'll never get over her. Even if he thinks they might have divorced, the fact that she died means he will never get over any of this.*

Oren met Rose's gaze and asked, "What do you want?"

Rose stuttered with surprise. "What do you mean?"

"Exactly what I said. You're twenty-one years old with the rest of your life ahead of you. You don't want to be a babysitter for the rest of your life. But what do you want? How do you want to fill your days?" Oren asked. His tone was urgent. Wild.

Rose knew she couldn't answer sarcastically. She couldn't be silly about such a serious topic.

So she said, "I just don't want to go back to Mississippi."

A smile fluttered across Oren's lips.

"What do you want?" Rose asked, throwing the question back. "You're only twenty-seven."

"Only twenty-seven," Oren repeated as though he couldn't believe it. "I feel like I've lived seven thousand different lives."

"Only seven thousand?"

Oren's smile widened. He shifted off the desk and approached her. Rose's nose was filled with his musk, the smell of smoke, patchouli, and oak. Her heart pumped. *This is the romance I've always dreamed of. This is the beginning of everything.*

Suddenly, his arms were around her waist. She was pressed up against him.

"I want a future," Oren affirmed. "I want children. I want a wife."

Rose's eyes filled with tears. This was exactly what she'd yearned for him to say. It was hard to believe this was happening—just two months after she'd met him. Just two months after his wife had died.

He couldn't have killed his wife. It was impossible.

Not this man. Not this man she was falling head over heels for.

Suddenly, his lips were upon hers. Swiftly, the world shifted off its axis, and Rose's eyes were closed, and she was wrapped up in his arms. Suddenly, nothing she'd ever known made sense to her anymore, and this was all she'd ever understood.

* * *

Rose and Oren kept their romance a secret from the Waldens and Zachary. Rose was tentative, and Oren agreed that it might "frighten" the Waldens to know that Oren was seeing their babysitter.

"Everyone thinks I'm off my rocker right now," Oren said tenderly one night when they were wrapped up in each other's arms in his study, their minds swimming with whiskey and love. "I don't want them to think you're a part of some kind of mental break. When the time comes, I'll tell them. When the time comes, we'll leave the place and make a real go of it."

What could Rose do but trust him?

Rose's love for Oren gave her a newfound purpose. She'd never felt this way before. Her hours with the children sizzled with magic; she was funnier, prettier, and more talkative with the other employees at the Walden Estate. Baxter and Miriam both told her there was a "light" in her.

"You're glowing, honey," Miriam explained. "You're infectious."

Rose spent her days off with Oren. They couldn't get enough of each other. By late September, they were clumsier about their arrangement and spending long hours in the Nantucket Historic District. Although they didn't dare hold hands or touch, Rose knew how close they'd become. It was apparent to every passerby.

On one of these afternoons, she spotted Officer Sean Slagle across the street from where she and Oren ate ice cream cones.

It was startling to see Sean out and about like this. Ever since that first kiss she'd shared with Oren, Rose had convinced herself that the fire didn't exist, that Natalie had never been Oren's wife, and that Rose was the only woman Oren had ever loved.

But the way Sean Slagle looked at them now brought it all back.

"Those clowns," Oren said now, guiding Rose away from Officer Sean. "They don't have anything on me. They haven't even come around to ask questions in weeks. But they still look at me like I'm a monster in some German fairy tale. I can't take it."

Oren gave Rose a look that meant she needed to play along.

Rose said, "It's awful. It's so obvious you had nothing to do with what happened."

Rose had stopped herself from saying *the fire*. It sounded too violent.

Oren took her by the hand and led her farther away from Sean, rounding the corner and diving into a little restaurant where the cheapest plate of food cost fifty-two dollars. Oren grabbed a table in the back and ordered the fanciest wine Rose had ever drunk, plus a cheese plate that made her think back on the Kraft singles she'd grown up with and laugh. Had Oren ever eaten such cheap food? She imagined not.

Oren took both of her hands over the table and kissed her knuckles. His eyes were like saucers. "I don't know what I would have done this year without you," he said. "You've saved me."

Two days later, Rose received a letter at the Walden Estate. This was a surprise to everyone, as Rose's family hadn't sent her anything all summer long, and she'd hardly spoken with any of them on the phone. *They're happy I'm gone,* she'd reasoned already. *They had too many kids to keep track of as it is.*

The letter had no return address. Rose took it to her bedroom and tore it open to find a brief note from Officer Sean Slagle.

Rose,

Please stay away from Oren. Although we can't get him behind bars this time, it's clear to all of us at the station that he's dangerous.

Let me know if you need help getting out of your current situation.

Come by the station any time on your day off, or call my home phone number, which is listed below.

Sean

Rose folded the letter and returned it to its envelope. Her first thought was to get rid of it. God forbid Oren found it and thought she was sneaking around on him. But her second thought was: *how dare he?* She hadn't agreed to go out with Sean, and now Sean wanted to make unfounded accusations about the man she loved. He wanted to "save" her from the happiest she'd ever been. He didn't know anything about her! He just assumed!

She knew Sean was just jealous. That had to be it.

But she couldn't let Sean's jealousy destroy her life.

After the children went to bed that night, Rose snuck back to Oren's and considered telling him about Sean's letter. But she imagined Oren would fly off the handle, so she kept quiet. Maybe being in love meant knowing what to keep from your lover to ensure his happiness. Perhaps it was all a balancing act.

Autumn continued, bringing storm clouds and questions from the Waldens about how much longer they wanted to stay on the island. Did they want to go back to the city? Did they want to try out California? A teacher joined the staff for the school year and took up many hours of the day with the children, which allowed Rose beautiful mornings and afternoons with Oren. It was remarkable to her that nobody in the Walden family had caught on yet. Or, if they had, they'd decided they didn't care.

Even Zachary was too enmeshed in his personal affairs to notice Oren's newfound commitment.

Rose wondered if everything would go on like that for

months and months. She wondered when they would have to make a decision and reveal their hand.

But then, time had its way with them.

In October—just four months after they met—Rose discovered she was pregnant with Oren's child.

Everything changed after that.

Chapter Fifteen

Present Day

Rose's newfound obsession with Natalie snuck into her nightmares. She found herself in a burning room with Natalie as Natalie tried to tell her something in a language Rose didn't understand. *"What is it?"* Rose begged her in her dreams. But Natalie couldn't say anything before she collapsed on the ground.

What does she want me to know? Rose woke up thinking.

It wasn't that Rose believed in ghosts. But something about the Grayson Estate and Natalie's story haunted her. She had to get to the bottom of it.

The fact that Sean was back in her life felt proof of that, too.

Rose was in her kitchen nook with a mug of coffee and a scone. It wasn't yet seven, but her head thrummed with questions. For whatever reason, she wanted to look up Natalie's obituary again. She hadn't seen it since June 1993. She hadn't seen it since *before* she'd decided to believe in everything Oren was, everything he stood for.

I fell in love with him, and he ensnared me. Was Natalie ensnared, too?

But the Nantucket newspaper didn't have anything that far back online. It was pre-internet. Another time.

Rose went for a seven-mile run, showered, and then drove downtown to the Nantucket Records Office. She'd never actually been there before, but she'd read online it was a haven for every bit of paperwork Nantucketers had left behind: marriage certificates and moving addresses, proof of death and birth. She parked and went into the chilly basement to find the man in charge of the collection bent over his desk, wearing a thick pair of reading glasses. He started when he heard her behind him.

"I'm sorry to startle you!" Rose smiled.

Jeremy removed his glasses and waved his hand. "It's no trouble. I get so immersed in the past down here. I was several decades away."

Rose remembered, now, that Jeremy was the husband of Alana Copperfield, which meant he was the brother-in-law of her friend, the woodworker Charlie. Rose reminded him of this connection, and Jeremy beamed.

"Charlie and I have bonded like crazy this summer," he said. "My daughter just went up to Manhattan to 'seek her fortune on Broadway,'" he explained with air quotes, "and I haven't really known what to do with myself. But Charlie and I discovered tennis, and we're getting better and better."

It was hard for Rose to imagine Charlie on a tennis court rather than in his woodworking studio. It seemed so active for a man so ponderous and artistic.

"What can I help you with?" Jeremy asked.

Rose raised her chin. She couldn't beat around the bush. Not with something like this.

"I want to look at someone's death certificate," she said, grateful her voice didn't shake. "Is that possible?"

"Did this person die in Nantucket?" Jeremy asked.

"Yes."

"Do you know the approximate death date?"

"June 16, 1993."

Jeremy hopped to it, routing around the aisles of file cabinets, guiding Rose on a scavenger hunt. June 1993 was near the wall. Rose reminded herself to breathe.

"Her name was Natalie Grayson," Rose said. "Quinne was her maiden name."

Jeremy gave her a look, which meant he knew *exactly who that was*. He'd probably been in high school at the time of the fire. It must have been right before the major car accident that had caused him to lose his football scholarship to Notre Dame. *He has a past, too.*

Jeremy flipped through the death certificates from June 1993. Rose waited with bated breath. She could imagine how devastating it would be to hold the certificate in her hands—proof of the terrible thing that she'd allowed herself to ignore for the entirety of her marriage.

I'm sorry, Natalie.

Jeremy flipped through them a second and a third time, then looked Rose in the eye. "Are you sure you got the date right?"

Rose was taken aback. "It couldn't have been any other date."

Jeremy let his arms hang. "It's not here."

Rose gaped at him. How was this possible? *Maybe somebody stole the death certificate,* she thought.

"Do you have newspapers from that week?" she asked.

"We have every newspaper published in the past one hundred and fifty years," Jeremy announced proudly, guiding her to another section of the chilly basement. "You're sure it was June 1993?" he asked. There was an edge of doubt to his voice.

"Yes. No question," Rose said firmly.

It didn't take long for Jeremy to find the obituary for Natalie Quinne Grayson. It was just as Rose remembered it, with that same photograph from so long ago.

Rose thought, *She was so beautiful. I didn't realize it back then. I was twenty-one, and Natalie seemed so much older than me. At twenty-six! She was still a baby.*

How foolish I was!

It was my foolishness that led Oren to me.

"But why isn't the death certificate here?" Rose asked after a long pause.

Jeremy's expression was difficult to read. He leaned back, his lips twisting. "She was married to Oren Grayson?"

Rose nodded. She searched his eyes for some sign that Jeremy knew she, too, had been married to Oren Grayson. But everyone knew that. Didn't they?

"Oren Grayson has more money than God," Jeremy said.

Rose's heart stopped beating. "What are you saying?"

"I'm saying that anything can be printed on the paper," Jeremy said. "You can fake an obituary easily. You just have to throw money in the right direction."

Rose was speechless. *It's impossible.*

"You don't understand," she said. "I married Oren

shortly thereafter. Natalie died in that fire. It completely affected our marriage. It affected my life."

Jeremy raised his hands. "I don't know. All I know is, there's no death certificate."

"But doesn't that just mean it was lost? Or stolen?"

Jeremy looked doubtful.

"Give me a minute," Rose said. "I have a phone call to make."

Rose hurried upstairs to call Officer Sean Slagle. He sounded surprised when he answered the phone. Rose remembered when he'd urged her to call him all those years ago. *Now's the time.*

Rose didn't want to explain everything over the phone. Sean said he'd be at the records office in ten minutes but appeared in seven. His cheeks were pink. He was nervous.

Sean was just as flabbergasted about the lost death certificate as Jeremy and Rose. He asked numerous questions about how the certificates were stored and whether it was possible that it had been misplaced. But Jeremy said no.

That was when Jeremy had the idea to look through hospital records. He had a friend up at the Nantucket Hospital who was willing to dip into the files they had on-hand.

The three of them waited in the sun outside the records office as Jeremy's friend went through hospital records from thirty-one years ago. It was clear to all of them that Natalie would have been brought to the hospital after her rescue from the fire. That was how things went.

But the friend called back within the hour to say,

"No. We don't have anything here for a Natalie Quinne or a Natalie Grayson."

Sean's face was deathly pale.

"But you must have seen those certificates when you were looking into her death?" Rose suggested. "Back in '93? When you were going after Oren?"

Sean shook his head. "No. The Waldens and the Graysons kept everything from us. The entire investigation was like moving through a jungle at night."

Jeremy, Sean, and Rose stood in the sun. Confusion marred their faces. Eventually, one of Jeremy's employees came out to ask his advice about something—an email to a higher-up, and he said goodbye and, "Keep me in the loop."

This left only Rose and Sean. They gaped at each other.

"Jeremy thinks Oren paid someone at the paper off," Rose burst. "He thinks the obituary was a fake."

"That's insane."

There was electricity in Sean's eyes. It was proof that he wanted to chase this story to the ends of the earth.

"Let's go back to the Grayson Estate," he urged. "It's like you said. Maybe that diary was just the tip of the iceberg."

Rose drove Sean back out to the estate that afternoon with the windows cracked and her hair flowing out behind her. Rose fought her instinct to touch Sean's hand, there where he had it stretched out across his thigh. She told herself her emotions and hormones were all over the place. It was a result of the investigation.

Back at the Grayson Estate, the construction workers were taking a break outside and discussing the specifics regarding the ballroom rooftop and the "insane task" it was to ensure it was stable—that it could continue to have any kind of life. They stopped talking when they realized Rose and Sean were approaching. A few workers popped up, adjusted their hard hats, and said hello.

"Don't worry," Rose said. "I'll stay out of your hair." She chewed her lower lip, then added, "I'm not terribly precious about that old ballroom rooftop. If you say it has to go, it has to go."

With that, she breezed through the front entrance of the Grayson Estate with her heart throbbing in her throat. Sean was hot on her heels. She could feel his eyes through her back.

To clarify, Rose paused on the staircase, hand spread across the railing. "I don't want them to think I'm precious about this place. I wanted to retain as much of its glory as I could. But I don't want to cling to old ideas. I don't want to uphold anything dangerous."

Overtly, she was talking about the roof and the mansion and its numerous rooms and numerous antiques and artwork. But she could see it in Sean's eyes. He knew she was talking about Oren, too. About her memories. About the man she'd once loved—who'd poisoned her, the way a worm poisons an apple.

They returned to Natalie's room and went through the rest of the desk, dresser, closet, and the drawers beneath the ornate bed. There were more diaries, but most of them were from Natalie's girlhood, the time before she'd met Oren. One of them spoke of Natalie's fiancé at the time she'd met Oren. It was clear from Natalie's writing that she'd been head-over-heels for Howard. She'd been bright-eyed, youthful. She'd never thought to dream she'd die in a house fire one day.

There were photographs, too.

The photographs were particularly harrowing—especially for Rose. In them, Natalie and Oren were sensationally beautiful, arm in arm or kissing on a beach or sitting in a convertible with sunglasses on. Natalie showed a sillier side, sticking out her tongue to Oren, who looked moody, his eyes glinting.

Sean touched Rose's back and breathed, "Are you all right?"

Rose realized she hadn't said anything in more than an hour. She'd been immersed in Natalie and Oren's life pre-Rose.

Rose picked up the photographs of Oren in the convertible, Oren at the baseball field, and Oren at the racetrack. Her eyes stung with tears. "He looks just like he did when I met him," she said.

Sean bowed his head.

I wonder if he's still jealous? Rose wondered, then cursed herself for thinking it. How could he be jealous of a wanted murderer? How could he be jealous of the heinous man who'd destroyed Rose's life?

But of course, Oren had been and probably still was the sort of man who always got the girl he wanted. Sean wasn't that kind of guy.

Not until now, Rose thought, then scrubbed it out immediately.

"I guess it's no surprise you fell in love with him," Sean said, as though he read her mind. "Look at him."

Sean sounded sorrowful.

Rose stuttered and closed the album where they'd discovered the photos in the first place. "You have to understand. He had so much power over me."

Sean nodded. He held her gaze. It was as though he

was waiting for Rose to say something else, to explain herself even more.

But Rose didn't want to tell Sean about the baby. She didn't want to tell anyone about the baby.

Even the Salt Sisters didn't know.

Chapter Sixteen

October 1993

Oren took the news just as Rose dreamed he would. He was ecstatic, leaping from his desk chair to wrap her in his arms and spin her in a circle. He then put her down gently on her tiptoes and kissed her lips, her fingers, her forehead, and her stomach. There were tears in his eyes. Rose thought, *This is the happiest day of my life.* It was only the hundredth time she'd thought that since she'd met Oren. She figured there were hundreds of thousands more.

That night, they lay in Oren's bed and talked about the future in a way that made it feel real for the first time. Oren propped his head on her stomach as his eyes swelled.

"I hope you'll marry me," he whispered. "Make it official."

Rose brought her hands on either side of his face and had to stop herself from screaming with joy. Instead, delicately, softly, she said, "I want to marry you, Oren Grayson. I want to be with you the rest of my life."

Oren bought her a ring a few days after that. Over dinner on her day off, he got down on one knee and slid the ring over her finger. Rose wept and threw her arms around him. They were alone at a beautiful beach house on the opposite side of the island—far from the prying eyes of Mr. and Mrs. Walden. It was the first night they were able to pretend they were "husband and wife" rather than two people bunking at the Walden Estate.

Rose knew she was days away from quitting her babysitting gig. She and Oren couldn't stay at the Waldens' after they confessed news of their engagement and the baby. Oren told her that night they'd move to this very beach house after she quit; from there, they'd plan whatever came next.

"The wedding has to be in Manhattan," he explained. "That's where most of my business contacts are."

Rose didn't hesitate; she didn't think twice about why it was so essential that his business contacts came to their wedding.

He told her the wedding needed to be sooner rather than later. "There's a ticking time bomb in your belly," he explained. "We don't want anyone to do the math and figure it out."

Oren drove Rose back to the Walden Estate late that night. In the dark car, she kissed him and promised she'd quit her job first thing tomorrow. His eyes glinted with the orange light from the Waldens' exterior lamps. He kissed her knuckles and said, "Good luck with Mrs. Walden. She can be a trip."

It sounded ominous.

Rose woke up early to tend to the children. She got

them up, fixed their breakfast, and ran them through the strict morning schedule prior to the tutor's arrival. At nine thirty, it was just her and Evie alone in the playroom, giving different voices to Evie's dolls. There was a loneliness in Evie's eyes, proof that she didn't love it when her brothers and sister went off without her. Rose wanted to tell her that "real life" would happen to her sooner rather than later. She needed to enjoy it.

Rose didn't get a chance to corner Mrs. Walden until after bedtime. She tiptoed away from Evie's room and hurried downstairs. If she thought about what she needed to do too much, she'd panic and put it off till tomorrow. She couldn't afford that. The Waldens needed to find a new babysitter. Rose needed to get on with the next phase of her life.

Would the Waldens be invited to their wedding? Would they care? Or would they only come because it was essential to be seen at such an event?

This was a world Rose didn't understand. Maybe she never would.

Rose knocked on the door. Behind it, she could hear Mrs. and Mr. Walden discussing something and listening to music. Zachary was gone—maybe in Rome, although Rose couldn't remember. Oren was, of course, at their beach house. *Their new home.*

"Come in!" Mrs. Walden sang.

Rose poked her head in to find Mrs. Walden's eyes glossy with a drink in her hand. Mr. Walden was on his feet, searching through a couple of records stacked on the side table. They looked bemused.

"Hi," Rose said meekly.

"This is a surprise," Mrs. Walden said, raising her glass of wine.

"Could I please talk to you?" Rose's voice wavered. "It will only take a moment."

Mr. and Mrs. Walden exchanged glances and shrugged. Rose stepped in. The air reeked of alcohol and smoke. Rose couldn't figure out which of them was smoking.

Rose remained standing. She shifted her weight nervously. Mr. and Mrs. Walden sat down in front of her. Rose was reminded of a job interview. *But this was an exit interview*, she reminded herself. It didn't matter what they thought.

"I wanted to thank you again for this opportunity," Rose stuttered, "but unfortunately, the time has come for me to move on."

Mrs. Walden looked stoic and dead-eyed. Mr. Walden turned to look at her.

"I know this puts you in a difficult position," Rose said. "And I'm sorry about that."

Mrs. Walden sniffed.

"Thank you for telling us," Mr. Walden said. It seemed as though he couldn't take the silence. "When do you need to go?"

"As soon as possible," Rose said, thinking of the baby in her womb. "But I know you need to find a new babysitter. I can be here a little while longer till then. Maybe two weeks?"

Mrs. Walden arched a single eyebrow. "Why don't you sit with us, Rose? Why don't you sit and tell us exactly what you're going to do next?" She smiled wider. "Why don't you sit and tell us just what, exactly, could be better than living at our multi-million-dollar estate in Nantucket?"

Rose's head swam. *Does she know about Oren? Can*

she see it written all over my face?

Or did she see me sneaking around? Has she known for months?

"Did some boy call you from Mississippi?" Mrs. Walden said.

Rose filled her lungs.

"I need a valid explanation," Mrs. Walden said. "Otherwise, I will not free you from your contract."

Rose was taken aback. *Free me from my contract?* Rose could just as easily pack her things and leave the estate tonight. She didn't have to tell Mrs. Walden anything. The other house staff could take care of the children for a while. What was the big deal?

And then the realization struck Rose at once. *She's drunk. She wants to play with me like a dog with a chew toy.*

What do I care?

Rose stuck her hand into her pocket to remove her engagement ring. She slipped it on her finger and extended her hand.

Mrs. Walden's eyes were enormous. Slowly, she got to her feet and reached for Rose's hand. "Where did you get this?" she rasped.

"I'm engaged," Rose said.

Mrs. Walden said, "But the ring. It must have cost a fortune." Her eyes glinted with intrigue. Her lips parted.

Silence filled the room. Rose tightened her fist to ensure Mrs. Walden couldn't whip forward and take the ring from her finger.

"Could you give us a moment alone?" Mrs. Walden said.

Rose shifted back, heading to the door.

But Mrs. Walden shot, "Not you. Rose, stay where

you are."

It was then she realized she was talking about Mr. Walden. Mrs. Walden wanted to be alone with Rose instead.

Rose remained in the center of the rug. Mr. Walden slunk from the room as though he'd done something wrong.

Rose forced herself to look Mrs. Walden in the eye. She refused to let her gaze drop.

Suddenly, Mrs. Walden was directly in front of her. Her nose was maybe an inch away from the tip of Rose's. She could feel her breath on her lips.

"You're a lot of things, Rose. But I never imagined you to be a con artist," Mrs. Walden rasped.

"I'm not a con artist."

"Tell me you didn't nab a job with a wealthy family just to spend more time with other wealthy people. Just to get yourself enmeshed."

"That isn't why I came here." Rose raised her chin.

"Who is it?" Mrs. Walden demanded. "Who's the lucky man?"

Rose thought, *Don't tell her. Don't give her any power over you.*

But then she heard herself say, "It's Oren Grayson."

Mrs. Walden's face burst into a horrible smile. Rose's blood ran cold. There was something in Mrs. Walden's eyes. But Rose couldn't read what was going on in her head.

"You think he's your ticket out of your social class, don't you?" Mrs. Walden breathed.

Rose flared her nostrils. "We're in love. I'm in love with him. It has nothing to do with class."

"It has everything to do with class," Mrs. Walden

blared.

Rose had never wanted to hit anyone before. She didn't want to now, either. But she understood the impulse more than ever.

"I didn't come here to manipulate Oren into falling in love with me," Rose insisted. "He was married when I arrived."

Mrs. Walden's eyes glinted. "That's right. And whatsoever could have happened to sweet Natalie? What a horrible *accident* that was!" She said it with heavy sarcasm. She said it as though Natalie's death had never been an accident, as though only idiots thought it was.

But Rose was of the staunch belief that Oren was innocent. He was the love of her life.

The back of Rose's neck was slick with sweat. She inhaled and exhaled. "We want to start over."

"He'll dump you, you know," Mrs. Walden said. "At the first sign of how weak you are, or how little you are, or how inconsequential your family is, he'll dump you for someone else. That's the kind of man he is."

Rose took a dramatic step back. All she wanted was to race through the house and whip into the chilly night. All she wanted was refuge from this horrible woman.

But Oren had left her here, and she didn't have access to a phone till tomorrow. She had to sleep here tonight. There was no surviving the chilly October air.

"I can help you, honey," Mrs. Walden said, adding honey to the horror she'd already shot. "I can get you out of this. We're planning to go to Manhattan soon. You can move with us. Start over there. You can enroll in a few classes here and there. We know people at Columbia. And the children just adore you. I can't let you go easily. Not when I see you destroying your life so plainly."

Rose couldn't help herself but say, "It's too late. I'm pregnant."

Because she hoped admitting to the baby would ease things between them. It would force Mrs. Walden to reckon with how "real" this was.

But instead, Mrs. Walden sniffed. "You'll regret this day for the rest of your life."

She then turned on her heel and whipped her hand toward the door, indicating it was time for Rose to leave.

Rose hurried out of the room, went upstairs, and wept into her pillow.

But she told herself, *It's over. I did what I came here to do.*

She had to be proud of herself for facing that horrible woman.

And she had to remind herself, *No matter how wealthy I become, I can never become like her.*

It was much sadder to say goodbye to the children. They'd been difficult and unruly, but she'd loved them to a degree. When Mrs. Walden requested that she leave the house as soon as possible the following afternoon, Rose packed up her things and hugged the children, promising that she'd visit as soon and as often as she could. Hamilton kicked her shin a final time on her way out, which felt fitting. To him, he was enraged she'd decided to leave, and he wanted to show that.

Just before she left, Rose sent a letter back home to explain what was happening—that she was going to get married and she was moving.

But it had been a very long time since she'd spoken to her parents. She wasn't sure how to tell them about the great and powerful events of her life.

* * *

Oren and Rose didn't remain in Nantucket long after Rose left the Waldens. The beach house across the island was beautiful but far too small for Oren, who was accustomed to big, sprawling homes or else enormous apartments at the top of ornate Manhattan apartment buildings. "You really must know Manhattan in the winter," he explained of the city. "It's wonderful."

So, by late November, they were in the city. Rose had never been before, and it captured her imagination. It felt beyond her wildest dreams. They ate at divine restaurants with Michelin stars; they ate at little hole-in-the-wall places with three tables and the "best-undiscovered chefs of the city." They redecorated Oren's apartment—a space, it turned out, where Natalie had never lived. Rose guessed that was part of the reason Oren was okay about bringing his new fiancée there. Natalie's ghost didn't haunt it.

Rose met with the "best prenatal doctor in the city" for her pregnancy. Everything was right as rain. She was six weeks along, but the doctor promised she probably wouldn't start showing until five or six months because she was so tiny.

That meant it was time to plan a wedding.

Oren's idea was to have the wedding on New Year's Eve. "I used to have parties every year on New Year's," Oren explained one night in their living room. Out the window was Central Park, spread out like a fuzzy blanket. It was sunset. "Maybe we should make it a surprise. I'll invite everyone. We'll get the party started. Then you'll appear in your white dress, and everyone will understand what's what." Oren snapped his fingers as though this was the single greatest idea he'd ever come up with.

Rose was swept up in it.

A few weeks before their wedding, Rose turned twenty-two. Oren bought her an exquisite birthday cake— one that looked more like a wedding cake. They ate it and gazed through the window at the sprawling city. Because of the hormones, Rose felt perpetually on the brink of sobbing. Sometimes, she hugged Oren and said, "I'm so happy. I don't know what to do." Oren laughed at her and held her.

Christmas meant hanging out with Oren's brother, Zachary. Their parents had died many years ago. Zachary had a new girlfriend; one Oren talked badly about as soon as they left that evening. "Zachary never knew how to get himself a good girl," Oren scoffed.

Rose beamed. This was proof that *she* was a good girl. She was exactly what he wanted.

The wedding was just as sensational as Oren had said it would be.

Hundreds of people milled into the venue Oren had rented in Midtown—a place decorated with art nouveau stylings, forty-five circular tables, and dark shadows lit up with orange lamps that seemed taken from another era. Rose watched from above, already in her wedding dress, her makeup and hair done. She had to wait for her cue. She watched Oren shake people's hands and whisper in older women's ears, making them laugh. She watched the Waldens enter, though they'd left their children at home. Mrs. Walden was wearing something sensational and all black. Did she know this was Rose's wedding? Or did Mrs. Walden think Oren had already kicked Rose to the curb?

Oren's cue was taking the microphone and saying hello. "This has been one heck of a year for me," he said as everyone raised their glasses of champagne to him and settled in their chairs. "I can't tell you the wide range of emotions I've gone through. But through it all, I knew I had my marvelous family and friends. I thank you." He raised his glass higher. "I have to admit, I haven't been completely honest about this evening."

Guests turned to twitter to one another curiously. *What does he mean? Oh, Oren. He's always so tricky, isn't he?*

Rose took her bouquet downstairs and perched in the doorway, watching Oren.

"My life flipped upside down," Oren said. "I lost someone very dear to me. Someone I will never forget." He pressed his hand over his chest and made a forlorn face.

Rose thought, *He's faking his sorrow. He loves me so much more than he could have ever loved her. Doesn't he?*

"But I also met someone else," Oren said. "Someone who knows me, who knows my heartache, who knows my soul."

Suddenly, the five-piece string orchestra swelled from the corner. Lights came on in the corner and darkened elsewhere. More lights came on to illuminate a sort of "aisle" between the tables and chairs. Rose's throat spasmed with panic. But she clung hard to her bouquet, fixed her face into a smile, and walked down the aisle just as she'd practiced that morning. She tried not to glance to either side. But when her eyes shifted, she couldn't help but notice how different the crowd's emotions were. Some were emotional. Some were panicked. Some looked stricken. But Rose continued to the front of the room to link her arms with Oren, raise her chin, and recite her vows.

Within fifteen minutes, she was officially Rose Grayson. The crowd was on their feet. More champagne was poured, but Rose didn't drink a single glass. She placed her hand on her lower stomach gently and smiled at everyone, shifting through the crowd as Oren thanked everyone for coming. Rose was never required to say anything except "Thank you," "Oh, it's so nice to meet you," and "Oh, isn't your dress so nice?"

She came upon Mr. and Mrs. Walden near the far wall. Mrs. Walden gave her a kiss on each cheek and said, "Darling, you look perfect. Doesn't she look perfect, Oren?" But her smile was so sinister that Rose wanted to run away from her.

"Mrs. Walden hates me," Rose whispered when she and Oren walked away.

"Don't be silly, darling. Mrs. Walden hates everyone. But she hates herself most of all," Oren assured her, then kissed her ear.

It wasn't till after the fireworks blasted through the night sky over Manhattan that Oren dipped Rose into a kiss and whispered in her ear: "What do you say we spend the next few months in Paris?"

Rose's eyes bugged out with surprise. "Paris?"

Rose had never envisioned herself in Europe.

But she'd already known Oren long enough to understand that when Oren wanted something, he got it. He had a vision for Paris. And Paris was where they were off to.

Rose was already in over her head. She just didn't know it yet.

Chapter Seventeen

Present Day

Rose drove Sean back to his police car later that afternoon. Sean carried a box of "potential evidence" regarding the Oren and Natalie investigation that contained journals, photographs, and personal items. Rose could only think, *Natalie never thought her private things would be gone through like this. She never thought her diary would be evidence for her murder.*

Rose cut the engine and gazed at Sean through the dying cerulean light. It was suddenly strange to her that she hadn't seen him around so often in the past several decades. She'd hardly left since 2004. Where was he?

She asked.

"I left Nantucket for a while," Sean admitted. "I met someone; I wanted to try to make it work. She wasn't an islander, and she convinced me there would be more upward mobility career-wise if we went somewhere bigger."

"How did you like that?"

Sean sniffed. "For a long time, that was my life. We had a couple of kids. We had bills to pay, windows to wash, and cars to take care of. We went to bed every night and ate breakfast every morning."

Rose searched through his words for some sign that he'd loved her. But what did love really mean?

"I didn't know she was cheating on me," Sean admitted finally. "When she confessed, I was blown over. I had no idea she was so good at lying."

Rose felt it like a knife through the heart. She wet her lips. "Did you leave immediately?"

Sean shook his head. "No. I think forgiveness is an essential part of every relationship. I wanted to go to therapy. I wanted to talk about everything. I even asked her a bunch of questions about the guy, just so I could fully grapple with the situation. She was up for it at first. But after a couple of months, she said she couldn't respect me anymore."

Rose's jaw hung open. *Respect?*

"She said she would have preferred if I'd gotten angry," Sean said with a soft laugh. "She wanted me to, like, punch a wall or something."

Rose's hands were clammy.

"Maybe it was a test I failed," Sean said. "But I don't blame her, and I don't blame myself. We grew apart over the years. That kind of thing happens all the time."

Rose's eyes filled with tears. "You're right. It happens all the time."

"Maybe it doesn't even have to feel that sad?" Sean suggested.

But Rose wasn't so sure. There was tremendous

tragedy in life. She'd been around long enough to reckon with that.

Sean said goodbye and wished her a good night. "It was one heck of a day," he said before he closed the door between them.

Rose returned home. She felt frantic and strange and got undressed as soon as she entered her bedroom, pulling on a ratty T-shirt she'd had since Mississippi. She felt like herself in it. Then she poured herself a glass of wine and went out onto the veranda to call Hilary. Before she could, though, her client's name filled the screen.

"Hi! How are you?" Rose's voice was overly bright. How could she have forgotten about the stolen sculpture? It hung above the rest of her life like a guillotine blade.

"I have to admit," her client said, "I'm not terribly happy about this robbery. We both know how much money I've already put down."

Rose groaned and rubbed the back of her neck. *It's always one thing after another.*

"I want to give the cops a little more time," Rose said hesitantly. "But otherwise, I'm happy to make you a new sculpture. It'll just take a bit more time." *A lot more time,* her brain added.

The client grumbled and said something like, *"I should have hired Bobby Bilton."* That stung. Rose knew Bobby Bilton's work. It was derivative. It also sold very well.

She'd lost work to Billy before.

Rose called Hilary after the client got off the phone and told her what they'd learned today at the records office and in Natalie's room. Hilary listened, captivated, then urged Rose to take care of herself.

"Of course," Rose said.

"I don't like that you're playing around in his territory again," Hilary said. "I'm sure he can sense you messing around where you don't belong."

"I literally bought the estate," Rose reminded her. "I didn't even buy it from him."

"I doubt he likes that, either," Hilary said.

Rose rolled her eyes, grateful that Hilary couldn't see her, then made an excuse to get off the phone and watch television inside. It had been ages since she'd zoned out, and it felt wonderful to forget about everything for a while.

Of course, it all came crashing back into focus when she turned off the television again.

* * *

It was one thirty in the morning. Rose's phone lit up with a message from Sean. Rose's heart slammed to a stop. She sat up in bed and blinked at the cold light of her phone. It had been a long time since a man had written her in the middle of the night.

SEAN: I think I figured something out.

SEAN: Can I come by tomorrow morning?

ROSE: Yes.

SEAN: Do you like donuts?

ROSE: Isn't that the old police officer cliché?

SEAN: Do you want donuts or not?

Rose giggled at her screen.

> ROSE: I love donuts. Who doesn't?

Sean appeared on her front stoop at eight thirty the following morning. Rose had already been awake since five, vacuuming and scrubbing kitchen counters. She had no idea what Sean had "figured out," but she guessed it was another piece of this elaborate Oren puzzle.

She was right.

Sean set himself up at the kitchen counter and spread out the donuts: caramel, chocolate, vanilla, and maple, all filled with cream. Rose's blood sugar shot to the heavens after just one bite. She poured them both cups of coffee and settled in beside him.

Sean had a few photographs with him. All of them had been taken from Natalie's room.

"Do you know who this man is?" he asked.

The photograph he was talking about was of a nineteen or twenty-year-old Natalie with a man a few years older than her, with long, slender arms and long brown hair. He looked a little like a rocker.

"No," Rose answered. "But Natalie wrote about her boyfriend before Oren. It must be him?"

Sean bowed his head.

"Oren always said he 'stole' Natalie from some guy," Rose said. "It must be him?" She searched her mind for a name from the diaries, then came up with, "Howard? I think?"

"Howard Reynolds," Sean affirmed. "Do you know that name from anywhere else?"

Rose squinted and took a bite of a donut. Her mouth

filled with cream. She repeated his name a few times but came up dry. "Where is it from?"

"You bought the estate from him," Sean said.

Rose gasped. "Of course!"

How could she have forgotten? The Salt Sisters had researched him very soon after Rose bought the estate. He lived in Manhattan and worked in importing and exporting, whatever that meant.

He was Natalie's first boyfriend.

It has to be a clue.

Rose pressed her hands to her ears. Her thoughts whirred and whirred.

"I got to thinking," Sean was saying. "It didn't make sense that the old Grayson Estate sat empty like that for so many years. Why didn't the owner do anything with it? Why didn't they refurbish it or bulldoze it?" Sean shook his head. "I couldn't understand it, so I dug deeper into Howard Reynolds and recognized him from some of her photographs."

Rose puffed out her cheeks. "You're a regular Sherlock, aren't you?"

"Ha. I wish." But Sean's smile was proof of how proud he was.

Rose pulled up the same images of modern-day Howard the Salt Sisters had discovered. She placed her phone directly beside the old photograph and sighed.

"He was so cute," she said. "Now he just looks wealthy and mean."

"I talked to someone from his hometown last night," Sean said. "Howard and Natalie were high school sweethearts. Apparently, it was a total shock when the two of them broke up. But the old friend didn't know the details.

He just said, 'Howard would have done anything to get Natalie back.'"

Rose raised her eyebrows. "Is it possible that Howard was the one who killed Natalie? Maybe he was jealous and set their house on fire?"

"It's certainly possible," Sean admitted. "It sends us down another path."

"But it's an exciting path," Rose said.

She hated to admit it to herself, but she still didn't like to fully acknowledge that Oren might have killed Natalie. Rose had loved Oren. Some of her still wanted to believe there was goodness in him and that she wasn't *wrong* for having fallen in love with him.

"Oren always talked about how Natalie's boyfriend had been so awful. So bad for her," Rose whispered. "I remember feeling so proud that Oren was the kind of man who knew how to love women properly. I felt so protected." Rose's eyes filled with tears. "Gosh, I was so wrong!"

Sean touched Rose on the shoulder, and Rose smiled through her tears.

"Sorry. My emotions are all over the place," Rose said. She picked up a donut and took another bite. The sugar opened her mind a little bit. It reminded her of where she was and why. It reminded her of how much time had passed. *But it's good that it did. It's good that I'm not that person anymore.*

"I think we should go to Manhattan to meet Howard," Sean said. "I have so many questions I want to ask him. Why didn't he do anything with the estate? What did he think when Natalie left him for Oren? Did he and Oren ever meet?"

Rose's heart pumped. It was hard to picture herself in Howard's office in Manhattan. It was hard to imagine herself shaking his hand. *This was Natalie's first love. He's mourned her forever.*

Has Oren mourned Natalie, too?

"Let's go to Manhattan," Rose said, sounding more confident than she felt. "I'm ready when you are."

"I'll make plans immediately," Sean said. "Tomorrow?"

"Tomorrow," she affirmed.

Chapter Eighteen

January 1994

Oren and Rose reached Paris on January 9, 1994. Rose was three months pregnant and called herself "happily married" in letters she sent back to Mississippi—some of which she wrote on the private plane that took them across the Atlantic and slipped into a yellow mailbox at Charles de Gaulle Airport. Her wardrobe was nothing she recognized—a series of taupes and whites and soft blues made of exquisite fabric.

Oren didn't tell her that he owned his own place in Paris.

He kept it a secret, like so much of his life. But Rose was still of the belief that secrets between them were romantic. They brought a certain electricity to everything they did.

At the airport, Oren and Rose slipped into a taxi and whisked off to his place in the Saint-Germain-des-Pres on the Left Bank. The taxi driver opened her door, and Rose stepped out onto the sidewalk and raised her chin to see Notre Dame, little cafés with circular tables, gorgeously dressed people, and bakeries just about everywhere she looked. Rose hadn't yet started to gain real weight, perhaps because she was only twenty-two and three months into her pregnancy, but she was ravenous. She made a plan to eat from every bakery in their neighborhood. She made a plan to really live.

Within that first evening with Oren, Rose was captivated enough by the city to ask, "What if we lived in Paris for the rest of our lives?"

Oren cackled. "Why not?"

The apartment was sensational. It was much smaller than the one in New York, but because it was Paris, Oren said he didn't care. "What do we need all that space for, anyway?" There was a living room, a kitchen, a beautiful bedroom, a guest bedroom, a dining room, and a room that doubled as the library and study. Half of the books were written in French. Oren told Rose that he'd always wanted to get better at French, so Rose set to work learning so they could do it together.

"This is why I fell in love with you," Oren said. "You're the kind of girl to go after things. That's why you left Mississippi."

They lived that first week in Paris in a bubble of love, beauty, and joy. They ate everything. They slept in. Every late morning, Oren went out for croissants and fresh butter, and they ate in bed.

Rose felt her belly get slightly bigger. She felt sure she was going to pop from all this French butter.

"I want you big and pregnant and powerful and strong," Oren said.

Rose's heart cracked open with joy. She remembered

how judgmental her own mother had been about other people's bodies, including Rose's, and thanked her lucky stars she'd found someone who didn't care about that. Who wanted her healthy. Who wanted a big and bouncy baby.

Most afternoons, they walked along the Seine, as Rose had always read you were meant to when you were in love. They people-watched from cafés. Oren told her stories about growing up different fights he'd gotten into with Zachary, and Rose found herself sharing her own life in Mississippi—how difficult it had been to be the eldest of so many children and how she'd once begged her parents to "stop making more babies" because they were running out of food.

Oren took her hand and breathed, "You'll never go hungry again. I'll protect you and the baby forever."

It was January 20th already. Oren's friends were in town, and they planned to go out to Clown Bar, a sensational restaurant in the eleventh. Rose got ready in the guest room. She was getting better at matching the makeup of the French women she saw on the street every day. It was understated yet elegant. The dress she wore had an empire waist and flowed over the growing bulge so nobody could see it—not yet. But Rose was a little over three months along. Oren said it was nearly time to share with everyone. It was almost time to announce "the next generation of Graysons."

Oren and Rose took a cab to Clown Bar. It was raining and black and damp. They got out and met Oren's friends beneath a splendorous ceiling painted with old-fashioned clowns and detailed with gold. Rose was sure she'd met Oren's friends Barbara and Scott at the wedding, though she couldn't remember a single detail about them. It was clear they came from money. They had that smell about them. And there was something in Barbara's eyes that Rose had once recognized in Mrs. Walden's gaze. She was judgmental. She didn't believe Rose belonged. She never would.

Rose put on a false smile but felt her confidence shatter.

Rose's intellect and background were often put to the test that night. Barbara and Scott had read everything and traveled everywhere. They could speak on Greek politics from 1000 BC or cuisine in the Napa Valley or Japanese television stations. Nothing was out of reach.

By contrast, Rose knew very little about anything. She'd read a great deal, especially since coming to Paris, but most of what she'd read had been fiction. There'd been a lot of Jane Austen. Her cheeks flashed with heat.

Sometime after the third course, Barbara left to have a cigarette, and Scott excused himself to go to the bathroom. Oren took Rose's wrist in his massive hand and squeezed hard.

"You're embarrassing me, darling," he shot.

Rose felt it like a dagger. She stuttered and tried to pull her wrist away, but Oren was too strong. Anxiety filled her chest, and she found it difficult to breathe.

By the time Barbara and Scott returned, Oren had released her wrist. But there was a sharp red outline where his hand had been. It felt like a warning.

That night, Oren didn't bring up his embarrassment. But the way he looked at Rose was different. She felt like a dog that hadn't performed correctly at a dog show. She hadn't caught the Frisbee. She'd disobeyed.

That night opened a portal.

The abuse trickled in.

At first, it was just little things. A squeezed wrist. A sharp word. An insult that meant she *wasn't good enough, wasn't smart enough, couldn't possibly understand.* It got even worse when Oren realized that Rose's French was better than his already. When she embarrassed him at a café in the third because her French was lilting and beautiful and the barista said so, Oren smacked her on the street outside. The smack startled Rose out of her skin. She blinked at Oren, at this man she'd fallen head over heels for, and turned on her heel, hurrying away from him.

Oren ran after her, turned her around, and kissed her. "I just want you to respect me," he whimpered. "I just want you to love me most of all."

On either side of them, tourists and Parisians hurried past. They had places to go. They had things to do, people to love, and food to prepare. Nobody could really see the quivering young woman with the slightly pregnant belly. Nobody could see her tears.

Sometimes entire days passed by when Oren didn't touch her, criticize her, or smack her. Rose reminded herself of these on the bad days. *He's stressed because of the baby. Maybe we should go back to Manhattan. Perhaps we should go back to Nantucket. That's where we fell in love. Maybe our love is waiting for us there.*

A business associate of Oren's came to Paris in early February. He wasn't married, and Rose wasn't needed to "keep the wife company," so the men went out alone. Rose adored those nights to herself. She walked by herself through the shadows of this tremendous city. She shivered outside of cafés with cups of tea and fluffy croissants. She went to a few museums and wept openly in front of impressionist paintings. She couldn't believe how far she'd come in her life. Why was it she felt so alone? Was loneliness to be expected, no matter where you went or what you did? Was loneliness just a fact of life?

Why had she imagined her loneliness would die out the minute she fell in love? Why had she imagined loneliness was a fact of the poor rather than the rich?

That first night, Oren came home reeking of perfume. It didn't take an expert to make sense of what was happening. Oren's business associate wanted to be around beautiful women, so that was what they did. Rose pestered Oren about it. She asked him, "Do you really want to be with me?"

His face scrunched to a tight red ball, and he said, "How could you ask me something like that? Don't you know how much I love you? Don't you know what I've done so we can be together?"

The abuse continued. It followed them into mid-February. Oren's business associate remained in Paris, taking an apartment in a trendier district. Oren often spent the night there, leaving Rose to twist alone in their silk sheets and marvel at the weight in her chest. *At least he's not here to beat me,* she found herself thinking. She cursed these thoughts and reminded herself just how in love she was. Just how happy she was. *I'm in Paris! I'm in the most beautiful city in the world!*

Rose called Mississippi on February 13th.

It was the first time she'd dialed her parents' home number in three or four months. They hadn't been invited to the wedding. Rose sensed they were resentful, though they probably wouldn't have been able to afford the trip to New York City in the first place.

Rose's little sister answered. She snapped her gum and said, "Mom's here." She sounded like a brat. Maybe they all hated Rose now. Maybe they thought she was too big for her britches.

"Hello?" Rose's mother sounded obstinate. Rose could picture her in the glow of the television, maybe with a few chip bags beside her on the sofa. What time was it there? Rose quickly calculated to glean that it was nearly three in the afternoon in Mississippi and nearly nine at night in Paris.

"Hi, Mom." Rose's voice cracked open.

"What's the matter?" There was no tenderness here. Only intrigue. Probably, her mother wanted to laugh in her face.

Rose took a sharp breath. She told herself not to sob.

"What is it, Rosie?" her mother demanded. "Did you call just to breathe at me?"

Rose closed her eyes and pictured her mother's face—craggy from cigarettes with nicotine-stained teeth.

"Rose? Where on earth are you?" her mother asked.

"I'm in Paris."

"Well, well, well. How nice."

Rose sniffed. "I don't know what to do."

Her mother coughed and inhaled, proof she was smoking. "Is my daughter unhappy with the wealth she's fallen into?"

Rose was quiet. Her heart felt so bruised.

"Is my daughter ungrateful for the wonderful life she has?" her mother demanded.

Rose closed her eyes. Her head throbbed. It occurred to her she hadn't eaten much today. The baby needed nutrients. It needed proof that someone loved it out here in the open air.

"I'm not ungrateful," Rose breathed. "It's just that..."

"It's just what? You got out of here," her mother

reminded her. "You got out, and you're living high on the calf over in Paris. Tell me one reason I should feel sorry for you."

Rose hiccuped with sorrow, then smacked her hand over her mouth.

"I know. Boo-hoo," her mother sang.

"It's just that he's not very nice to me all the time," Rose hurried to say.

"You're saying the wealthy man you married isn't always so nice?" Her mother was condescending. "How surprising!"

Rose curled into a ball on the sofa and gazed out at the black night. Where was Oren right now? Probably with some French woman who took his breath away. Probably drinking wine and eating decadent food. They'd only been here five weeks or so, and already her marriage was off the rails. It had to be Rose's fault.

Oren was probably thinking he shouldn't have married her.

He was probably thinking, *I'm not over Natalie. I'll never be over Natalie.*

"I need help, Mom," Rose breathed. She sounded pathetic. No wonder her mother hated her so much.

"Honey, you need to learn to help yourself," her mother said.

Suddenly, there was a horrible twist in Rose's abdomen. She groaned and stretched out. Pain electrified her head. *The baby. What's wrong with the baby?*

Rose hung up without saying goodbye and limped across the living room. Her stomach spasmed. Pain was the only thing she understood. A few minutes later, blood dripped from between her legs, and she understood. *I have to get to the hospital immediately.*

Rose hobbled downstairs to hail a taxi. She felt stupid, especially when she cried and winced and smacked her thigh with pain in the back seat. The driver kept glancing back with worry. But every time he asked her a question, she couldn't answer. The stress made her French fly out of her head.

Perhaps it shouldn't have been a surprise that Rose lost the baby.

Perhaps it shouldn't have shocked her so greatly.

But one minute, she'd had all the ingredients for a happy life—a handsome husband, a baby on the way, and apartments in Manhattan and Paris and Los Angeles and Dubai. A fat bank account. A fresh wardrobe. And the next, she was twisted up in bloody sheets at a hospital in Paris, asking them to call her husband. "I don't know where he is," she yelped. "I don't know!"

Rose couldn't tell Oren about the loss of their baby until the following afternoon. She was released and took a cab back to their apartment, where she found Oren nursing a hangover and already sipping a glass of whiskey. She'd calculated the cost of each pour of that particular whiskey before. *Seven hundred dollars each.*

Oren was quiet for a long time after she told him what happened. He looked at her as though it was all her fault. Maybe it was. Perhaps this was Rose's body's way of saying *Get out of this situation. Get yourself back to America.*

But Oren wrapped his arms around her and held her as she wept. He cried, too.

They made promises that night. They told each other they would continue to try. A baby was in their future; they were sure of it; they'd already set so many plans. Oren was going to stay home more often; he was going to take care of his wife. And Rose was going to be better; she was going to be great. She was going to know everything there was to know, but she was never going to "upstage" Oren, especially not in front of his friends.

Being married was like a balancing act. In her post-miscarriage haze, Rose was so sure she could manage it. She could carry her and Oren and their love for the rest of her life. It would probably get much easier from here on out. Probably.

Chapter Nineteen

Howard Reynold's office was located in Midtown, Manhattan, in an art deco building that reminded Rose of the one she'd been married in just a few blocks away. *Memories always linger just beneath the surface. They're always apt to bite you.* Rose and Sean parked in an underground lot a block away and approached the building with their hands in their pockets and their chins raised to take in the mighty view. Around them, the city was alive in ways she'd forgotten it could be. People of every race and creed and fashion and knowledge whizzed past, some talking exuberantly into their phones, others crying, others hurrying to the bus or the subway. Some of them ate sandwiches like their lives depended on them. Some of them paused to take photographs.

It was incredible to Rose that she'd spent any portion of her life in Manhattan. It seemed so foreign to her.

Sean had made an appointment with Howard for

three o'clock. The secretary asked them to wait in the lobby and explained Howard was running late. She said it as though Howard was the most important man on the entire island. His time was precious, and Rose and Sean were stones in his shoes.

"Does he know why we're coming?" Rose asked Sean now, wringing her hands and watching for any movement from the closed door.

"He knows you're the one who bought the house from him," Sean said. "I think that intrigued him enough to take the meeting."

Rose's heart swelled. Every instinct she had told her to jump up and run to the elevator. *Stop digging into Oren's business. You know what he'll do to you. It won't be pretty.*

Suddenly, the secretary bolted to her feet, fixed her jacket, and announced, "Mr. Reynolds will see you now." She even opened the door to let them in.

Howard's office was decorated with Japanese minimalism in mind. Rose imagined that Howard had spent time in Japan and decided to bring back their aesthetic principles with the hope that some of their other sensibilities would rub off on him. That was the way of the wealthy. They wanted to simplify everything. They wanted to throw money at every problem.

Howard stood to shake their hands. He wore a cologne Rose recognized from her years with Oren, something that evoked money and the idea of multiple vacation homes. He was still handsome, but there was something overly slick about it.

Natalie's first love.

"Congratulations on your purchase of that dump,"

Howard said, smiling in a way that showed too many teeth. "What's your vision for the place?"

Rose's voice shook. "I'm thinking a hotel or a bed-and-breakfast."

"Right. Like Nantucket needs more of those." Howard's voice sparkled with sarcasm.

"On the contrary, more and more tourists come every summer. I think another bed-and-breakfast is just the ticket. And it's been a shame to watch that plot of land go to waste over the years," Sean affirmed, sticking up for Rose. He wasn't wearing his police officer uniform and had opted for a pair of slacks and a dark green sweater. He looked good. Understated.

Howard's eyes flickered as though he wanted to roll them. He folded his hands across his desk and looked at Rose. "How can I help you today?" He said it distractedly.

Rose filled her lungs, then took the plunge. "We want to know why you let the old place sit like that for so many years. Why buy a half-destroyed property and do nothing with it?"

"It happens all the time," Howard insisted. "My wife says I have too many irons in the fire. I had to take some out."

"But this particular place," Sean pressed. "It once belonged to Oren Grayson. Are you familiar with that name?"

"Only in as much as I bought the place from him," Howard lied.

His face was like a stone. It was time to bring out the big guns.

Rose reached for her purse and pulled out the old

photograph of Howard and Natalie. "We know that isn't true," she breathed, placing it on the desk between them.

Howard's bushy eyebrows shot up his forehead. The color drained from his cheeks. Slowly, he dropped his hand to take the photograph and raise it closer to his face. He looked captivated.

"Where did you get this?" he breathed.

All the air was taken out of the room. It was difficult to breathe.

"We're trying to get to the bottom of an investigation abandoned many years ago," Sean said after a pause.

"Natalie," Howard whispered.

Rose nodded. "We don't think it was an accident."

"Of course, it wasn't an accident," Howard shot. "Oren Grayson wasn't the kind of guy who had *accidents*."

Rose thought of the miscarriage in Paris. *An accident Oren couldn't avoid.* But she wouldn't bring that up with Howard. She didn't even plan to tell him she was Oren's second wife.

Howard fixed his face and set the photograph down in front of him.

"We know why we think it wasn't an accident," Sean said. "But why don't you think it was?"

Howard snorted. It seemed difficult for him to keep still. "You should have seen the way Oren sauntered up to Natalie at the bar the night we met him. He had this air about him. Like he owned the world, but he was the kind of guy who got *whatever he wanted* from birth. He never had to work for anything in his life. Natalie ranted about him all night after he left. But I knew in the pit of my stomach that something was wrong. And not long after that, Natalie left me for him."

Howard chewed the inside of his cheek and turned to gaze out the window. It was as though he wanted to remind himself of all he'd earned. All he'd fought for.

"I kept tabs on Natalie after they got married," Howard said. "I felt like I owed it to her. She'd been hypnotized by Oren's wealth, his multiple homes, and all the adventures he could take her on. But I knew there would be a crash landing. I just didn't imagine it would end like that."

Rose's heart throbbed. She thought she might throw up.

"When I found out Natalie died in the fire, I went insane," Howard sputtered. "I got in my car and drove to Nantucket immediately to see the old place. I couldn't believe how massive it was. It looked haunted. Terrifying. I went into town after that and heard whispers from the islanders. They all assumed Oren had killed Natalie. They didn't know my background; they couldn't have known I loved Natalie, so they told me everything. They told me that they'd once seen Oren smack her upside the head in public. They told me that if you drove back to the mansion at a certain time of night, you could hear the married couple fighting. I was mystified. Why had Natalie left me for this outright evil man?"

In her chair now, Rose felt Sean's eyes settle on her. *Does he know Oren was cruel to me, too?* She wondered. She felt Howard was giving up pieces of her past through the retelling of Natalie's story.

"I wanted to stay and go to the funeral," Howard said. "I wanted to pay my respects to her family, whom I hadn't spoken to since Natalie left me. But when I inquired about the funeral, I learned there would be a *private memorial service.*" Howard used air quotes. "Why private? It didn't make any sense. I started my own investigation after that. I went to the police and pretended to be someone else. I gave a false name."

Sean twitched in his chair. Did he remember Howard now?

"But it was clear that the Graysons weren't cooperating with the cops," Howard said. "I became obsessed. I rented a little cabin and asked question after question of Nantucket locals. But I soon grew tired of their stories. They never gave me any more details than I already had. So I pooled together the rest of my money and bought the old Grayson Estate. It was the only way to see the life Natalie had lived. It was the only way to get to the bottom of it."

Howard's chin quivered. He looked on the brink of sobbing.

"I picked up the keys from the real estate agency and returned to my cabin. I wanted to mentally prepare, you know? I knew I was about to enter Natalie's tomb," Howard said. "I sat down with a beer and a notebook. I wanted to write all my thoughts down. I wanted to make sense of myself. But that's when the phone rang." Howard closed his eyes. "It was Penelope."

Rose and Sean exchanged confused glances. Who was Penelope?

"Penelope was a girl I'd been seeing before I ran away to Nantucket," Howard explained. "Somehow, she'd gotten my number. She wanted to know how I was. She was worried about me. Her voice brought me back to earth in an instant." Howard snapped his fingers. "I looked in the mirror and saw this man with scraggly hair and a bushy beard staring back at me. I realized the Orens of the world would always win, no matter what. Which meant I had to start playing by their rules if I wanted to get ahead.

"Everything happened quickly for me after that. I showered, shaved, packed up, and went home to Penelope. We were married within three months, got pregnant, and after that, I got the job that changed my life forever. The job that eventually brought me here."

He said it proudly, as though he'd gone to battle and come back victorious.

"What made you finally sell the old place?" Rose asked.

Howard shifted his gaze back to her. It was as though he'd forgotten she was there. "It's true that I held on to the property much longer than I should have. My wife didn't even know I still had it. But now? The memory of Natalie feels a thousand miles away. It feels like somebody else's life."

This time, Howard picked up the photograph and handed it back to Rose without looking at it. It was as though he'd convinced himself not to care about Natalie all over again.

"I hope you can prove what you're trying to prove," Howard said, dismissing them. "Natalie didn't deserve what happened to her. Oren was a sociopath. I truly believe that."

Howard pressed a button on his desk that called his secretary in. She smiled and said, "I'll walk you out."

It was a swift way of getting them out the door.

Rose and Sean were wordless after they left the office. Rather than return to the car immediately, they walked block after block. An exhilarating and fresh wind came through the tall buildings and blasted through their coats.

It was a reminder that autumn was just around the corner.

"Terrible guy," Sean said finally. It was the first thing either of them had said in more than forty minutes.

Rose burst into laughter and nodded. "Terrible."

"But he seems sure Natalie is dead," Sean said. "I was sort of hoping, you know, that her lack of death certificate meant that, well..." Sean wet his lips. "It sounds stupid."

"Meant she wasn't dead?" Rose offered. "I've been hoping that, too."

"But she would have reached out to Howard. Right?" Sean asked.

Rose raised her shoulders. "Maybe she wanted to get rid of all the men in her life and start over."

But even as she said it, her heart thudded with sorrow. It was tremendously unlikely that Natalie had gotten out of this alive.

"You want to get a cup of coffee?" Sean asked. He stopped short in front of a diner, one that reminded Rose of the diner they'd gone to back in Nantucket.

"I'm starving," Rose admitted. "Mind if I get something to eat?"

They sat at a red booth and ordered fried fish sandwiches with mayonnaise, crispy lettuce, and red onion, plus onion rings to share. Rose sipped her Diet Coke and studied the interior, which was just black-and-white photographs of celebrities who'd eaten at the diner, plus several of the Rat Pack during a forgotten time. Rose had never been here even though it wasn't so far from where she'd once lived with Oren.

"This must be painful for you," Sean said suddenly, breaking her reverie.

Rose turned to meet Sean's gaze. She knew he was

talking about Oren's abuse. She knew, too, that he was too much of a gentleman to ask if it had happened to her, too.

"I realized I don't blame myself anymore," Rose said suddenly, surprising herself.

Sean cocked his head.

"I used to blame myself for all of it," Rose breathed. "I blamed myself for falling for him. I blamed myself for giving up my life goals to follow his. I blamed myself for signing a prenup that destroyed my chances of a second life after he left me. And I blamed myself for 'making' him cheat. No matter where I looked in my story, I felt guilt."

Sean shook his head sadly.

"Maybe that guilt won't ever fully go away," Rose said. "But Howard's right. Oren was a kind of sociopath. I would have done anything he asked me to. He manipulated me. It happens to millions of girls across the world every day. And I'm just so grateful I got out."

Sean reached across the table and took her hand. Rose didn't flinch away.

"I want to avenge Natalie for what happened to her," Rose whispered. "It could have been me."

"We'll find a way," Sean said. "I promise."

Chapter Twenty

T he rest of Rose and Oren's marriage went like this.

Immediately after Rose's miscarriage, they tried again. And again, and again. But when Rose wasn't pregnant by the end of spring, Oren decided it was best that they pack up and move back to Nantucket. "The fresh air will do you good," he suggested. He didn't want to go to the doctor to see if anything was wrong. He was convinced it was Rose's body. He was convinced he was powerful and strong, able to impregnate anyone at any time. Rose bit her tongue from saying *Natalie never got pregnant. Maybe you're the problem.*

Oren bought them an incredible home on the bluffs of Siasconset—just three miles from where he'd once lived with Natalie and a mile and a half from the Waldens. Rose decided she didn't care about that. She decided to throw herself into redecorating their luxurious home. She'd never lived anywhere half as gorgeous and had never had such a dense bank account to play around with, and she ordered just about every luxury item she could think of—chandeliers and top-quality mattresses and ornate rugs and sofas that were both regal and terribly soft. She wanted to make a home where Oren would fall in love with her again.

But Oren seemed distracted. Did he have another woman?

Rose felt sure she would get pregnant once they were in Nantucket, and she wasn't wrong. By autumn, she was pregnant again. Oren was overjoyed. It was practically the same scene as last year. Oren picked her up and whirled her around in a circle, then they talked for hours into the night about how excited and in love they were.

The miscarriage came earlier this time. Rose was grateful for that. At least she wasn't already in her fourth month.

That rhythm carried on for many years. Rose got pregnant five more times after that for a total of seven pregnancies. None of them were viable, no matter what she did. She stayed in bed. She took supplements. She lost weight. She gained weight. When she finally did go to the doctor, they were stumped about why she couldn't keep a pregnancy. They suggested she was stressed, and she insisted she'd never been happier in her life.

She was getting really good at lying to everyone, including herself.

Oren hit her exactly six times between 1995 and 2001. Three of those times, he hit her in the face, then sobbed and sobbed, telling her he loved her, telling her that he wouldn't know what to do without her. Rose always comforted him. Rose always told him it would be all right and that it wasn't his fault.

She knew he wanted a child so badly.

167

Rose lived in fear of one of his mistresses giving him what she couldn't.

Rose was thirty-two years old when Oren announced he wanted a divorce. They were on the veranda of their Nantucket home with a roasted chicken set between them. Rose was thinner than she'd been in years, having worked diligently at Pilates and eating very little all winter. Now that it was finally spring, Oren had decided he was done "messing around in a life he didn't even like." Rose crumpled. She raced to her private room and locked the door behind her. She fell to the floor and sobbed and sobbed as quietly as she could. All she could think about was Natalie. Was this what had happened before Oren set fire to the house?

He didn't set fire to the house. He didn't kill Natalie. I've known him for eleven years. I would know if he murdered someone.

Wouldn't I?

Oren was gone by the time she left the room.

Rose stayed in the Nantucket house by herself for a little more than a week before she hired a divorce lawyer and decided to figure out the next steps. The prenup dictated that she got nothing. She got nothing despite offering eleven years of emotional support, eleven years of love and tenderness. It was as though she'd been a piece of furniture in his life. He'd decided to throw her out.

"At least you don't have children," said a friend over the phone. "That would make everything so much more complicated."

Rose hung up the phone immediately and decided she was done with Oren's society.

She remembered, now, what Mrs. Walden had said

about Oren's class. *You'll never fit in.* Rose realized she never really had.

Mrs. Walden had been right.

Not long after, Rose was waiting in her divorce lawyer's office. She knew she was about to get kicked out of Oren's place—their place—and she was at the end of her rope. But a blond woman sat across from her, doing a crossword. She looked normal. She had a little less money than she needed, but she made it all right. Something about her felt familiar to Rose.

So Rose asked, "Are you getting divorced, too?"

The woman raised her chin and smiled. "My friend is. I'm just here to help her."

"That's nice of you," Rose said. Something about the woman's eyes electrified her. "I wish I had a friend who would do that." She laughed nervously, then added, "I was the kind of woman who threw herself totally into the marriage. What a dummy, right?"

The woman tilted her head. "I don't think that makes you dumb. I think it makes you romantic. Who doesn't want to feel a little romance now and again?"

Rose smiled. She couldn't remember the last time someone had offered her such tremendous kindness. She told herself not to burst into tears.

"I was married, too," the woman confessed. "It ended terribly."

"It feels like we're too young to have all this life experience," Rose said.

"You're telling me," the woman said.

Rose sniffed. "What's your name?"

"I'm Stella. You?"

"Rose."

Hilary Salt left the lawyer's office a few minutes later

and introduced herself. Rose felt the pieces of her heart slowly shifting back into place. She agreed to meet with them for drinks and dinner at Hilary's place, and not long after that, she moved in with Hilary—into a sprawling mansion that was even bigger than Oren's place. Hilary had more money than she knew what to do with, but she wasn't mean-spirited about it. She'd been through the metaphorical wringer of life. And she was eager to talk about it.

As Rose slipped deeper into this marvelous life of kindness, friendship, and good conversation, Hilary and Rose worked diligently around the house, painting walls and redesigning rooms. Hilary told Rose she had an artistic eye. Rose had never really thought about it that way. She realized she'd only ever seen herself as a part of a greater whole rather than an individual.

"You should give it a try," Hilary suggested.

Hilary sat for Rose's painting not long after that. Rose worked hard on that first portrait, digging into Hilary's personality and the specific details about her face that made *Hilary Salt* who she was. When Rose was finished, Hilary was smitten and hung the painting in one of her rooms.

"Keep going," Hilary begged. "You owe it to yourself not to stop."

Rose moved into her own dinky apartment not long after that. It was the tiniest place she'd ever lived in. It was also the first place she'd ever been able to call her own.

It was a start.

It was a breath of fresh air.

It was time to live.

Chapter Twenty-One

Present Day

Rose invited the Salt Sisters to the Grayson Estate three nights after she returned to Nantucket from Manhattan. She wanted to show them her very own haunted house. And she wanted to tell them how much they'd been on her mind lately—specifically Stella and Hilary, who'd saved her life.

She practiced it in her head. *I always thought men were the ones who had to save women. I never knew women could save each other. Not until you two walked into my life.*

I didn't deserve you. I still don't understand how I got so lucky.

It was a beautiful day in August, just south of seventy-five degrees. Rose set up a few picnic tables across the grounds and hired a private chef to grill sensational barbecue chicken on the grill she brought from home. Because some of the construction workers groaned with hunger during the chef's prep time, Rose ran out to grab more ingredients to feed the construction workers, too. She didn't want anyone to feel left out.

"Guess what?" One of the head construction guys approached with his hat in his hands. He looked cute, his hair slightly greasy on top, his face and arms tan from all the hard work.

"What's up?" Rose smiled.

"We figured out a way to save the ballroom roof," he said. "Want to come check it out?"

Rose followed him through the back entrance all the way to the ballroom. Rose hadn't entered that area of the house in quite a while, and she was amazed at the amount of work they'd finished. It was beginning to look like something out of a storybook. They'd even managed to save the ceiling paintings of the starry night sky.

"You can walk under it safely," the worker explained. "We secured everything. Look." He gestured toward pillars they'd built along the edge of the ballroom. The pillars were delicate and beautiful, reminiscent of French castles. Rose took a hesitant step into the ballroom and raised her chin. Beneath her feet was a sparklingly clear marble floor—one they'd apparently discovered under mats Oren or somebody had laid down after they'd abandoned the house.

"It was really in better shape than we thought," the construction worker explained now.

Rose blinked back tears and imagined tourists here as early as next summer. She imagined their laughter and conversation in this very space—a space where, once upon a time, a young woman named Natalie had laughed and conversed with Oren.

Natalie's dead, Rose reminded herself now. *Don't get your hopes up.*

"Rose?" Hilary's voice echoed through the ballroom.

Rose twisted around and watched as Hilary strode through the ballroom and sidled up beside her with her eyes on the ceiling. Rose took Hilary's hand. For a moment, Rose imagined herself at thirty-two—broke and lost and nearly homeless. Hilary had said: *Why don't you move in with me?* And now, their lives were entirely different, but they were still themselves. They were still the best of friends.

They would always be the Salt Sisters.

"It's sensational," Hilary said now. "I can't believe I've driven past this place thousands of times and never knew what the inside looked like."

Rose pointed toward the far edge of the ballroom and said, "I imagine a big table right there next to a table with the best view of the water. That's where we'll always sit. You and me and all the Salt Sisters."

Hilary blinked rapidly. It looked like she was fighting tears. "You've had a difficult few weeks, haven't you?"

Rose sniffed. "I just don't know what to make of any of this."

Rose briefly explained their trip to Manhattan. She talked about her strange "fantasy" that Natalie was still out there somewhere. "Maybe Oren forced her to go somewhere else? Perhaps he pushed her out?" she speculated. "Maybe he just wanted to create a sob story about his wife. About his past. Perhaps it was all a manipulation tactic to get someone like me under his control."

Hilary cupped her elbows and raised her chin again to gaze at the ceiling. It was truly sensational. It was difficult to look away from.

"You shouldn't rule any of it out," Hilary said finally. "Not with Oren."

Rose's heart seized. She'd half expected Hilary to tell her to drop it, to remind her that they lived in the real world, where real rules applied.

But Hilary didn't do that.

Instead, Hilary said, "You might want to look into hiring a private investigator."

Rose tilted her head with surprise.

"I know. You wanted to be the private investigator," Hilary teased her lightly. "But there's so much about this world you can't know. It's so deeply entrenched." She spread out her fingers.

Rose knew Hilary was right. Hilary was from wealth. She understood the intricacies.

"I don't want you to get in over your head," Hilary said. "But you have money, now. Your own money. There's no reason you can't throw money at the problem and figure this out."

Rose's heart opened up. She remembered how strange it had been for her to learn that wealthy people just threw money at their problems to make them disappear.

Rose would never be as wealthy as Hilary or as Oren or as Mr. and Mrs. Walden. But she had enough for a private investigator. And she thought she owed it to herself—and to Natalie's memory—to pursue this. She'd already bought the Grayson Estate, for heaven's sake. This was her life's work.

"I have a recommendation," Hilary said, reaching into her pocket to find her phone. "She's brilliant. Lives in Manhattan."

"Why do you know a private investigator?" Rose asked with a laugh.

"You don't want to know," Hilary said.

"You'll tell me later?"

Hilary raised her shoulders and gave Rose a funny smile. "Maybe. Maybe not."

Rose received a text message from Hilary, filled with the details for the private investigator. *Vicky Smith.* Was it her real name? It didn't matter.

The other Salt Sisters arrived a few minutes later. They were overjoyed to be there, swallowing Rose in hugs. Rose tried to tuck all ideas about the private investigator into the back of her mind. But by the time they were on their second glasses of wine, Rose couldn't take it anymore. She fled to the other side of the estate to send Vicky Smith an inquiry.

She wrote: **I need to find Natalie Quinne Grayson. She apparently "died" in 1993, but there's no death certificate to speak of, and the funeral seems fishy. They didn't allow anyone to attend.**

For background, I married Natalie's husband not even a year after she "died." I was very young. I hope you won't think too harshly of me.

Money is no issue.

Rose stared at the message for a full thirty seconds before pressing send. She gasped, then hurried back to the table, where Katrina was doing an impression of a musician they all liked, and all the Salt Sisters were howling with laughter.

It was the first night of fun the Grayson Estate had seen in many, many years.

Rose knew it was the beginning of something incredible.

Chapter Twenty-Two

Rose woke up at five thirty the following morning to seven missed calls from Sean. She shot up and stared at the phone to read:

PLEASE CALL ME BACK ASAP. I don't care what time.

Did he mean that? It was difficult to tell. But Rose's phone was already against her ear, and she was listening to Sean's brrring. She imagined it vibrating next to his pillow, wherever he slept.

Suddenly, she imagined herself in bed beside him, listening to the sound of his breath.

Stop. There's so much else to think about.

It was chilly outside and black and sorrowful. It was hard to believe that she and the Salt Sisters had had a barbecue at the Grayson Estate just last night.

She needed to start calling it the Carlson Estate in her mind. She'd taken her maiden name back immediately after her divorce. It suited her—even if her family back in Mississippi didn't. It certainly suited her far more than Grayson had. *Rose Grayson* now sounded so foreign to her, like a language she'd once been able to speak that had filtered out of her memory.

Sean answered the phone on the third ring. He didn't sound groggy. "Rose," he said without saying hello. "I can't believe it. We found your sculpture."

Rose's heart slammed against her rib cage. Before she knew it, she was out of bed, her free hand in a fist. "You what? How? Where?"

Sean sputtered. "That's the strangest part of all. We used artificial intelligence technology to scan through thousands upon thousands of art auctions and online art fairs. It flagged an upcoming auction in Manhattan. I checked the photograph. It's yours. It has to be. But it's credited to another artist. Here, I'll send you a link."

Rose's blood boiled. She opened the link Sean sent to see a photograph of her gorgeous sculpture, the piece she'd spent so much of the year immersed in. On the auction website, it read:

You're invited to the party of the year. August 30th, 2024. Twenty-five iconic pieces of art will be sold at auction. Tickets are five grand to enter.

Rose's eyes widened with shock. "Five grand to enter?"

"It's for the Manhattan elite," Sean said.

"What do the Manhattan elite want with my sculpture?" she demanded. "I mean, don't they already have enough art? Enough Manhattan-based artists? It doesn't make any sense."

Sean seemed stunned with silence.

Suddenly, all Rose wanted was to tell him to come over, hold her hand, and tell her what to do.

But she didn't want a man to "save her." Not anymore.

Rose pulled the phone away from her ear and clicked through the website a bit more. Who were these people? How had they gotten her sculpture?

That was when she spotted who was throwing the event in the first place.

"Sean," she breathed into the phone. Tears filled her eyes. "Sean, I don't know what to make of this."

Sean sputtered. "What? What's going on?"

"Sean, it's the Waldens."

Sean was silent for a moment. "Remind me who they are again?'

"Mr. and Mrs. Walden," Rose said. Tears streamed down her cheeks. "They hired me to babysit their children thirty-one years ago. They're throwing the party. They're auctioning off my sculpture!"

Sean was speechless. Rose walked to the window and opened it wider to inhale salty sea air. The world was spinning too fast. She thought she might faint.

Why do the Waldens have my sculpture? Are they trying to punish me for something? Is Mrs. Walden finally going to get revenge for my departure?

Sean's voice came through the phone. "When was the last time you saw them?"

Rose's heart thudded. The memory dropped down from the sky. "It must have been 2001 or 2002," she said. "I was in Manhattan with Oren."

What Rose didn't say was *That was right after my final miscarriage. That was right after I fully gave up trying to get pregnant.*

"But that was years ago," Rose breathed.

Suddenly, an idea smacked Rose over the head. *Oren is involved in this.*

Oren is the one who took my sculpture.

She wasn't sure why it was suddenly so startlingly clear.

But Oren was probably aware that she'd recently bought the Grayson Estate. He probably wanted to mess with her. He probably wanted to keep her from digging through his things.

It's a warning, she thought.

"I can get a warrant immediately," Sean said over the phone. "We can be in Manhattan by this afternoon."

"No," Rose said.

Sean took a breath. "What do you mean?"

"I want to do this differently."

Sean sighed. She imagined he was thinking: *She has no idea how police work operates. She's in over her head. She's arrogant.*

But maybe because Sean was a kind and considerate man, he took a deep breath and asked, "What did you have in mind?"

Rose pinched her lips together. A plan formulated in her mind. Could she trust Sean with her idea? Then again, who else could she trust?

"I'll tell you," Rose said, "but you have to promise to keep an open mind."

"I promise," Sean said. "Whatever it is, I'll help you. As long as it isn't a crime."

Rose set to work late in the morning on her strategy. At the kitchen table with a cup of coffee and a bunch of jitters in her stomach, she dialed the phone number for Mrs. Walden's philanthropic organization. Mrs. Walden began the organization in the late 2000s to donate funds

179

to lower-class neighborhoods in greater New York City. Rose knew it was also a way for the Waldens to expense their cash. Nothing the wealthy did was ever selfless.

A secretary answered. "Thank you for calling The Walden Group. How can I help you?"

Rose put on her brightest and shiniest voice. "Hello! My name is Brenda Sparrow. I'm the portraitist hired to paint Mrs. Walden. Would you mind passing me through to her office phone? I recently purchased a new phone and unfortunately lost all of my contacts."

"Mrs. Walden isn't in today," the receptionist said, "but I'd be happy to pass along her number."

It was too easy.

Within a minute, Rose had Mrs. Walden's personal cell phone number. She didn't hesitate and called immediately. But Mrs. Walden wasn't the sort of woman who answered calls from numbers she didn't recognize. This left Rose with the terrifying decision of whether to leave a voicemail.

She decided to go for it. What else could she possibly lose?

"Mrs. Walden," Rose said, her voice musical, "my name is Brenda Sparrow. I'm a professional painter of portraits of the Manhattan elite—those I feel make a true difference in our iconic city. A friend of yours recently mentioned you as a potential candidate for my project. The paintings will be featured in an exhibit at the MOMA later this year. Please call me back and let me know if you'd be interested in sitting for your portrait. We'd love to include you in the exhibition, but time is limited."

Rose hung up and winced. She'd said "a friend of yours" without mentioning a name. It was fishy. It was risky. Why would Mrs. Walden trust a strange message like this?

But Mrs. Walden herself called before noon.

"Brenda Sparrow!" Mrs. Walden's voice soared. "You'd like me to sit for a portrait for the MOMA? What a sensational idea."

Rose's heart thrashed. *It was too easy to manipulate a rich person. You just had to tell them how important they were. Just as important as royalty.*

Mrs. Walden didn't even ask who'd recommended her.

After all these years, hearing Mrs. Walden's voice sent a chill through Rose's spine. It made her feel twenty-one again and fresh-faced from Mississippi, hopeful for a future she didn't know how to build.

It didn't surprise her that Mrs. Walden didn't recognize her voice in return. Probably, Mrs. Walden hadn't thought about her at all in years.

But why does she have my sculpture? Did Oren give it to her? Did Oren himself sneak into the house?

Questions spun in her mind.

Rose felt outside of her body as she secured a time to paint Mrs. Walden's portrait for August 25th, just five days before the party where her sculpture was set to be auctioned off.

"I'm looking forward to meeting you," Mrs. Walden sang over the phone. "I've always wanted to sit for my portrait. It's finally time."

Rose called Sean back and explained when she was needed in Manhattan. "But I told her we'd meet in my studio," she said after a dramatic pause. "Which means I need to head to the city immediately and rent one!"

Sean laughed. "You're a regular con artist."

"I grew up thinking these rich folks could walk all over me if they wanted to," Rose said softly, tugging at her hair. "I'll never be one of them. Not really. But I'm going to march in there and prove myself to them. I'm going to march out with my sculpture."

"If only you could carry it," Sean said with a soft laugh.

"It makes things difficult," Rose agreed. "But we'll manage it."

"We will."

* * *

The Salt Sisters were not pleased with Rose's plan. They begged her to be careful; they begged her not to go.

Hilary called as they drove to the ferry and opened the conversation with, "Just send Sean! He'll arrest them!"

"They're too wealthy," Rose explained. "They'll slip through my fingers. An alias allows me to see them for who they really are without giving myself away. And I need to figure out what really happened with Natalie. If I get deep enough, maybe I can get someone to confess something. I don't know."

"Just be careful," Hilary begged. "We want you back home as soon as possible."

Rose and Sean drove to Manhattan, stopping frequently for cups of coffee or little snacks from the gas station. The air sizzled with their anxious energy. It was hard to believe Sean had agreed to come with Rose already—a full week before the event where her sculpture was set to be auctioned off. But Sean insisted it was all a part of the investigation. He'd even cleared it with his boss at the station.

Sean parked his car and hauled their suitcases upstairs to the hotel they'd rented for the week. It was just three blocks away from the studio Rose hoped would be hers for the portrait and just five blocks from where Mr. and Mrs. Walden would host their party the following Friday.

Rose and Sean had rented separate hotel rooms. The receptionist gave them a curious smile as though she wanted to ask them what their story was. *Weren't they a couple?* But of course, that was just Rose projecting.

It was only three thirty. Rose had an appointment with the true owner of the art studio at five, which gave her and Sean a bit of time to relax in their separate rooms. Rose collapsed on the cloud-like bed and spread her arms and legs out as far as they could go. The air-conditioning was on high, and she felt chilly after sweating during the walk from the car. The August humidity was killer in the city. It was the reason so many people left during August. But she knew the Waldens were having this party at the end of August as a way to welcome so many people back for the beginning of autumn. School was set to begin. Real life plodded ahead.

The studio was exactly what Rose had envisioned for her "trap." The ceilings were fifteen feet tall with windows that nearly stretched all the way from top to bottom, and there were easels and primed canvases everywhere. Paint was flung into all corners, and paintings she could pretend were hers hung at strange angles. She'd already primed a canvas for her portrait of Mrs. Walden. She set that up on an easel, then positioned her paints and brushes on the table beside it. She was so immersed in her vision that she almost forgot Sean was still with her.

When she turned back, she found him smiling softly and watching her.

"Oh! I'm sorry," she said. "I got carried away."

"Don't worry about me," Sean said. "I've just never seen you at work before."

"By contrast, I always see you when you're working," she said.

It was the nature of their relationship, after all. She'd called. He'd come to help.

"I want to take tonight off," Sean admitted, palming the back of his neck. "What do you think about that?"

Rose raised her chin. A flush ran through her. *This is his way of asking me out.*

She knew it in her bones. She knew it as clearly as she knew Oren had something to do with her stolen sculpture.

"I think I'd like that," Rose said.

They went out to a French restaurant that evening and ordered escargot—which Sean had never enjoyed nor even thought to order. Rose showed him how to eat them properly; she refilled his glasses of wine; she laughed at his jokes and little stories. By the end of the evening, their hands were interlaced over the table, and they were gazing into one another's eyes.

It was eleven thirty at night. They'd already been at the restaurant for four hours. Only one other couple remained, and they were looking at their phones, ignoring one another.

It was as though the magic of the restaurant was only for Rose and Sean.

"I wish I could take back what happened all those

years ago," Rose breathed. "I wish I would have gone out with you instead of him."

Sean raised his shoulders as though to say *it is what it is.*

But Rose got out of her chair and pressed her lips against his. Her heart raced; her ears rang. His hand found the divot between her neck and her shoulder, and his thumb traced her collarbone. It surprised her. His touch was wonderfully tender.

When their kiss broke, their eyes were swollen and filled with tears.

It was clear to both of them that they wouldn't need two hotel rooms. Not tonight. Not for the rest of the week.

Rose thought, *I've never fallen in love as an adult before. Not really.*

It's better than I ever could have imagined.

Chapter Twenty-Three

Sean insisted on being there for Mrs. Walden's portrait. "It's not safe," he said. "If she figures out who you are at some point during the portrait painting, she'll flip out on you."

Rose was grateful for Sean's honesty and support. Her heart sang when he was around. At the breakfast table of their hotel restaurant, they held hands and ate bagels, gazing into one another's eyes. They'd been a "couple" for just a few days, and Rose felt as though she floated from room to room, as though everything she said and did was extra magical, as though New York City had opened its arms to them.

Of course, everything could turn on a dime. Rose was always aware of that. It was the nature of time.

But she found herself trusting Sean more and more as time went on, rather than less. She wasn't used to that, either.

Rose and Sean walked to Rose's makeshift studio and arrived an hour before Mrs. Walden was set to. The fact that she'd agreed to come to Rose's studio, rather than forcing Rose to come to her home, was proof that she really, really wanted her portrait painted. She really, really wanted to be in the MOMA. Rose chortled. Mrs. Walden's self-obsession would never fade.

But maybe it would take a hit this week. Rose hoped so.

Rose had set up a little area for Mrs. Walden to sit in the corner of the studio, where light spilled in from the window and would illuminate her face. Rose planned to paint Mrs. Walden as beautifully as she could as a way to get on her good side. With the skills she'd gleaned during her years as a professional artist, she felt sure she could get the painting done in a matter of six or seven hours. She'd let Mrs. Walden go after four and finish up the rest after she'd left.

That was the plan, anyway. Rose hoped it would work.

Mrs. Walden arrived just on time. Sean pretended to be a studio employee and led Mrs. Walden up the elevator and into the studio, where Rose wore a pair of overalls and had her hair in a high bun. Rose braced herself. Maybe Mrs. Walden would look at her and immediately recognize her. But it had been so many years since they'd seen one another. Rose knew she didn't look the same.

Mrs. Walden, of course, looked remarkably the same as she had thirty-one years ago. She'd thrown money into her face, and it had paid off. She glistened and glowed. She also looked slender yet powerful, a result of Pilates or yoga or some secret third thing rich people didn't let poorer people in on yet. She raised her chin and inspected the artist before her.

"Barbara Sparrow," she said. "It's lovely to meet you."

Rose smiled and shook Mrs. Walden's hand. She hadn't recognized her. Good.

"Thank you for coming all the way here," Rose said. "Please, sit down. Make yourself comfortable."

Mrs. Walden had opted to wear a regal-looking ocher dress. It suited her skin color divinely. It also made her look straight from the seventeenth century. She sat and adjusted her shoulders, then put her hands across her lap and raised her chin.

It had been years since Rose had painted anyone's portrait. But this was exactly how she might have positioned Mrs. Walden's face and body, given the chance. She dove right in.

Something was magical about painting someone's portrait. It was a little bit like digging around in someone's soul.

It was the closest two people could possibly be. But the person who sat for the painting was blind to that closeness. All they could do was be observed.

It was another two hours of painting before Rose got up the nerve to ask Mrs. Walden a question. "You've really done remarkable work for your organization. Tell me. When did you start?"

"It was 2008," Mrs. Walden said. "All my children had left the nest, and I needed something to do with my time."

Rose thought, *It's not like you raised them, anyway. Nannies did. Maids did.*

"How many children do you have?" Rose asked.

"Four."

Rose remembered their gorgeous faces back in 1993. She remembered how Evie had crawled into bed with her and immediately fallen asleep. Her heart ached to be needed like that. *I was never allowed to have my own.*

They continued making light chitchat about her children, about her grandchildren, about Mr. Walden and his numerous companies. It wasn't till later that Rose could reroute the conversation back to the foundation.

"And how do you raise money for your foundation?" Rose asked.

Mrs. Walden puffed her cheeks. "That's a difficult thing indeed. It's hard to pull money out of wealthy people's pocketbooks. But funny you should ask. We have an event this Friday. We're auctioning off works of art to the elite members of Manhattan society. The money will, of course, go toward the foundation. And it will pay the caterers and the bartenders and the party planners and so on." Mrs. Walden spoke quickly, whipping her hand in a circle.

Rose remembered that last night they'd spent together when Mrs. Walden had said, *You'll never belong.* A shiver went down her spine.

"Would it be possible for me to see the pieces being sold in the auction?" Rose asked. "As an artist, I'm always so curious about what's selling well and what people are making. I like to keep tabs on industry trends."

"Darling, I can't let you see any of them," Mrs. Walden said. "They're all locked away until Friday."

Rose's heart sank. She'd imagined being able to see her sculpture today. She'd probably been foolish to hope for that.

"Can I see my portrait yet?" Mrs. Walden said suddenly.

Rose hadn't anticipated this, but she fixed an easy smile on her face and said, "Sure. Like I said before, I'll need another few hours after you leave to finish. But it should be done by tomorrow."

Mrs. Walden got up and breezed across the room, a strange expression fixed to her face. Rose wondered if she was ready to rip Rose's painting to shreds.

But instead, Mrs. Walden stood pin-straight and looked at Rose's painting for a full five minutes without speaking. The air in the room was taut. Rose was too frightened to look at Mrs. Walden.

"It really is something," Mrs. Walden finally said.

Rose filled her lungs, searching for sarcasm in her voice. But Mrs. Walden's eyes were aglow. It was clear she'd never seen herself the way Rose had painted her: glowing, youthful, queen-like.

Mrs. Walden clasped her hands together. It looked as though she wanted to jump up and down. "I absolutely must show it off at the party on Friday!"

Rose's heart nearly burst. *This was all a part of the plan.* Mrs. Walden had walked right in.

"That can be arranged, I think," Rose said, sounding tentative. "The MOMA won't need it for another couple of weeks."

Mrs. Walden waved her hand from side to side. "If they make a fuss, let me know. I can make some calls."

Rose's heart swelled. She needed to make one last request. "How can someone attend the party? Does one require an invitation?"

Mrs. Walden's smile could have lit up a dark ocean. "Darling, I want to invite you myself. Here." Mrs. Walden ruffled through her purse to find an invitation for the event, which she slipped into Rose's hand. "I'll put you in contact with my assistant so you can bring the painting the day before the event. Make sure to wear something ravishing. You must do something about those bags under your eyes. And make sure to bring a handsome date. Someone in a tuxedo. These are the elites of Manhattan, darling. You want to appear as though you fit in."

Rose maintained a bright smile, one she hoped said *this is the happiest day of my life.*

Then she said, "I can't wait."

Chapter Twenty-Four

Rose and Sean spent all afternoon preparing for the fundraiser that Friday. Sean hadn't had a tuxedo—not even somewhere tucked away in Nantucket—which had required a shopping trip and a last-minute purchase, one that had made Sean's eyes bug out of his head. Rose understood. Sean's yearly wage wasn't much to write home about. But Rose hadn't come from wealth, and she had an incredible amount of respect for people like Sean. People who'd given their all to their communities. People who didn't save their cash just to prove they had a lot of it.

Rose bought a gown because she wanted to look pristine—just in case Oren was a guest. She had a hunch he would be. But she wasn't sure how much she could trust her gut.

Her gut had been wrong before, after all.

Sean and Rose waited in the hotel foyer. Sean looked captivated by her. He held her hand and said, "You're the most beautiful woman I've ever seen."

Rose snorted. "That's rich."

But Sean held her gaze. "It's the truth."

Rose's smile melted. She squeezed his hand and marveled, *Is this the fairy-tale ending I always dreamed of?*

But already, the car pulled up to take them to Mrs. Walden's fundraiser. Rose had wanted to come in style.

Sean opened the door for her, and Rose slid in and assembled the end of her gown around her ankles.

"It's showtime," Sean said, wagging his eyebrows.

Rose burst into nervous laughter.

The car reached the glorious art deco building thirty-five minutes after the fundraiser was set to begin. Already, wealthy and well-dressed men and women paraded from taxis and limousines and entered the gold-laced doors. Rose watched, hunting for some sign of Oren and the arrogant sway of his shoulders. But he wasn't among those entering. Maybe he wouldn't be here at all.

Sean had already told her as soon as she confirmed that the sculpture was hers, he'd make the call. A few cops were on standby in the area. The fact that she'd crafted this scheme was far beyond his scope as a police officer.

But she had to know if Oren was involved. She couldn't let him slip away. Not if he'd done something wrong. Not this time.

Rose slipped her arm through Sean's. He led her gently toward the doorman, who bowed as he opened the door. It had been a long time since a doorman had held the door open for Rose. Had the last time been when she'd been married to Oren?

Rose remembered so many doormen. So many of them had seen Oren verbally or physically abuse her. So many of them had witnessed an unhappy marriage. But they'd smiled and said, "Good evening, Mr. and Mrs. Grayson." They'd looked the other way.

Would Rose have looked the other way, too? Would she have said, *That's just the way things go?*

Rose handed over her invitation upon entering. The woman who took it looked it over, then smiled and said, "You must be the portraitist. You've really done something sensational. Let me ask you. Can I hire you to paint my portrait, too? Or is this something the MOMA must hire you for first?"

The woman's eyes glinted. Rose felt speechless.

"Really, honey. I'll throw as much money at this as I can," the woman said.

"Let's talk about it after the fundraiser," Rose sang, smiling.

"Of course," the woman said, fixing her face. "Tonight is all about the children."

"Yes. All about the children," Rose repeated.

After that, Sean and Rose entered a glorious ballroom. It was a bit like walking back in time. Chandeliers hung low from a bowed sky, glinting and throwing their light across the walls, and a full-string orchestra sat in the shadows. Music swelled. There was a ball in Rose's throat. She struggled to breathe.

That was when she spotted Mrs. Walden's portrait.

It hung far above their heads so that it seemed like Mrs. Walden gazed down upon them, formidable and wealthy.

Sean muttered under his breath, "You are so talented."

"I made her look the way she wanted to look," Rose corrected.

"That's still a huge talent," Sean told her. "You swindled our way in here."

Rose giggled, then fixed her face as Mrs. Walden

approached. She wore an elaborate ball gown, and her hair was piled into an architecturally bizarre set of curls and rolls on her head. But she really did look wonderful. Her eyes glistened strangely, though. It was proof she was already drunk.

She'd never been able to kick that habit, Rose realized.

For a moment, Rose allowed herself to feel tremendously sad for Mrs. Walden. It was clear something was very wrong with her. With her life. With the way she thought about herself.

"Darling, you made it," Mrs. Walden said, kissing both cheeks. "Everyone is giddy about the portrait. They can't get over it. Everyone wants to know your name. Barbara Sparrow. Barbara Sparrow. It's the name on everyone's lips!"

Rose blushed and glanced at Sean. Sean looked pale. It was clear he wanted to call his backup immediately.

Rose introduced him as her boyfriend, then realized it was the first time she'd ever said that aloud. Sean grinned and took Mrs. Walden's hand. But he didn't know what the wealthy did with other wealthy people's hands because he wasn't wealthy. So he shook hers. Mrs. Walden made a face and took her hand back.

Looking around, Rose spotted Hogarth Walden. He wore a tuxedo and drank something dark brown—a whiskey or a scotch, not unlike something Oren might have drunk. He'd grown up in this world, which meant he was a product of these people.

"I really would like to see the art pieces," Rose said.

"Of course. They're just that way," Mrs. Walden said, already growing bored. She moved on to someone else, and her voice echoed through the ballroom.

Sean and Rose cut through the throng of wealth,

sensational perfumes, and laughter that didn't sound terribly happy. Rose was careful to keep her eyes straight ahead. She wanted to confirm the sculpture was hers. She'd begun to grow frightened and wanted to get out of there. It felt as though her dress was too tight; she was struggling to breathe.

Sean and Rose entered the room where the artwork was held. Three guards stood on either side of the room, watching them with dull expressions. The auction was to be held later that night after everyone had gotten drunk enough to throw their money around, but the auctioneer was seated with a full glass of wine, clicking his jaw around.

That was when Rose spotted her sculpture. It was directly in the middle of the other artworks—sculptures, paintings, miniatures, busts, wooden carvings. Her heart leaped into her throat. She squeezed Sean's hand and walked up to it. It was out of her reach and oh, so heavy. Tears sprang to her eyes. She couldn't believe it was here. It was a piece of her heart and soul.

If Oren's not here, how did the sculpture get here? She couldn't get her head around it.

"We should call soon," Sean warned. Sweat billowed on the back of his neck. It was going to ruin his tuxedo. "I can't take this party for more than a few minutes."

Rose squeezed his hand. It was going to be difficult to leave her sculpture behind now that she knew it was really hers. But she knew it was necessary to have professionals deal with this.

"The bidding doesn't start till later," one of the guards warned them.

Rose set her jaw. "Thanks." She then twisted out of the room. Her breathing felt too rapid. She felt on the verge of a panic attack. She felt Sean hot on her heels and could see the phone in his hand he wanted to use to call in someone to help.

But that was when she spotted him.

That was when she saw Oren.

There he was. He stood in the middle of everything in an iconic tuxedo, his hair just as full and curly as ever, his shoulders just as broad. His smile was arrogant, sure, and he bowed forward to whisper a joke into the ear of the man he spoke to. Oren always liked to do that. He always wanted to make you feel "in on it."

Rose's knees quivered and threatened to give out.

This was the first time she'd seen him in years.

This was the man who'd ridiculed her, made her feel as though it were her fault that they couldn't get pregnant —he'd made her feel stupid and small and ugly.

This was also the man who'd given her everything. Who'd changed her life when she'd had nothing.

Tears filled Rose's eyes. She felt frozen.

Sean gave her a curious look, then followed Rose's eyes through the crowd. "Oh," he muttered because he recognized Oren.

It was no surprise that Mrs. Walden hadn't recognized Rose. She hadn't spent much time with her since Rose was twenty-one.

But the minute Oren looked in Rose's direction, Oren knew who she was. She wasn't Barbara Sparrow. She was his second wife.

Rose had come here to look in his eyes and see if he was guilty—for Natalie's death, for the theft of her sculpture.

She saw guilt there.

She saw rage.

And more than anything, she saw his singular belief that he could do whatever he wanted and get away with it. He thought he was above the law.

Rose's gut swirled with nausea. She thought she might throw up.

Sean was saying her name, but Rose couldn't look away from Oren's gaze. He downed his drink and set his jaw.

Suddenly, Sean was on the phone, muttering something. Rose couldn't remember who he was calling. She couldn't feel her feet.

Oren took a step toward her. He licked his lips. Beside him was a beautiful blond—much younger than he was. Was she his wife? Rose struggled to remember.

She still remembered marrying him. She still remembered giving her entire heart to him. How could she not have?

He manipulated me. He took me for all I had and left me to rot. I had nothing.

Suddenly, three cops tore into the ballroom, flashing their badges. The people at the front entrance had their hands up. They looked stricken.

"We're looking for Phil and Audra Walden," one of the cops bellowed.

The crowd parted to reveal Mrs. Walden. She looked just as powerful as she did in the painting, her eyes glinting. "What could this possibly concern, Officers?" She said it as though she planned to ensure every single one of them lost their jobs.

She probably could do that, Rose reasoned. She probably still would be able to, even if she was in the wrong. That was just how money worked.

The cop barreled toward her. Another followed him, while the third traced the crowd to find Sean.

"You are under arrest for suspicion of art theft," the first officer said to Mrs. Walden.

Mr. Walden appeared behind her with his hands up. He looked dopey. "I don't understand."

Rose turned to watch as Oren cut through the crowd, hurrying for the exit. Her heart slammed to a stop.

"It was him!" Rose screamed. "Don't let him get away!"

Suddenly, a fourth officer appeared in the doorway and slammed the massive golden door shut. Oren ricocheted and took off for another exit. But three cops were hot on his heels, surging toward him. Oren's escape strategy was akin to a child trying to get away with something. And it also proved his hands red.

Already, a cop had Oren's massive wrists in handcuffs. Oren cackled as though the whole thing were a game. His eyes found Rose's through the crowd.

"You think you can get away with framing me like this, Rosie?" he called.

Mrs. Walden gaped and followed his eyes. "Rose?" she whispered. "What on earth?" She then flailed her hand toward her and said, "She's an impostor, Officer. She pretended to be someone she's not!"

"Look at me, Rosie," Oren blared. "I did this for you, Rosie. For us!"

Rose's voice was meek. "You wanted me to be distracted. You didn't want me to find out your crimes."

"What crimes, Rosie?" Oren said as the cops dragged him out of the room. "Tell me one thing I've done wrong. Haven't I cared for you? Haven't I loved you till the very end? Wasn't it you who stopped loving me first, Rosie?"

He went on like that until they pulled him into the cop car. Rose could hear him screaming in the street.

Suddenly, Rose collapsed against Sean and burst into tears. He held her as she shook and cried, then led her out of the ballroom and into a taxi and back to the hotel room they now shared. He drew her a bath and held her hand as she trembled.

But already, the news was hot with Oren's arrest.

"Breaking! Millionaire Oren Grayson was arrested this evening under suspicion of art theft," a newscaster said, his face glossy and tan. "The New York City Police Department, in cooperation with the Nantucket Island Police Department, traced artist Rose Carlson's recently stolen sculpture all the way to the Walden fundraiser in Midtown this evening. What's particularly riveting about this story? Rose Carlson is Oren Grayson's second wife. We'll have more news at eleven."

There was speculation already that Oren had done what he'd done to "mess" with his ex-wife. To "teach her a lesson."

It was a surprise to Rose. She'd never thought anyone would be on her side. Not when Oren had money.

Maybe the tides really were turning for women.

Rose was wrapped in a robe and huddled against Sean in bed. She felt protected, soft. Already, she'd received word from her client, who'd texted:

> WOW. This is crazy. This art piece is going to be SO FAMOUS. And it's still mine!

But Rose wasn't so sure about that. She had a feeling she was going to give the client all her money back so she could keep the piece. She'd grown too attached.

"What now?" Rose breathed when the news went to commercial.

Sean laughed and kissed her forehead. "We can relax a little bit, maybe."

Suddenly, Rose's phone buzzed with another text. She assumed it was her client.

But instead, it was the private investigator.

She'd only written: **I found her. Here's her number. She wants you to call.**

Chapter Twenty-Five

The plane landed in Montana on September 8th. Rose was alone, her eyes out the window, watching the purple mountains come closer, closer. But the minute the plane dinged and settled, she turned back on her phone to field several messages from Sean.

SEAN: Good luck today.

SEAN: I can't believe any of this.

SEAN: What a crazy ending!

SEAN: I miss you.

The Salt Sisters had written their "good luck" as well. Rose sent them several heart emoji and got off the plane.

Rose had never been to Montana. It hadn't been high on Oren's list of places to go. Perhaps that was why Natalie had picked it.

Rose grabbed her suitcase and rented a car. Natalie had sent her an address, and she followed the directions to a T to get her to the ranch by five that evening. A yolk sun drenched the fields and valleys in orange light. It was so stunningly beautiful that Rose thought she was going to sob.

Rose drove down a long gravel driveway toward a little house at the edge of a massive property. Horses and cows milled in the middle distance. A tractor sat next to a red barn. It was nothing like the life she'd known. It looked like a painting she'd once seen in an art museum.

Rose got out of the car with shaking legs.

"Rose?" A beautiful voice came from the doorway.

Rose turned. And there she was.

Natalie Quinne.

Of course, her name was Caitlin now. Caitlin Rains.

Natalie wore a soft white dress, and her hair cascaded down her shoulders in grays and browns and blonds. She'd likely forgotten to get everything touched up and then decided not to care anymore. Her smile was the same as in the photographs of her, Oren, and Howard from all those years ago. Her teeth were white.

Natalie and Rose stood in awe of each other. Rose curled her hands into fists. She wanted to fall to her knees and apologize to Natalie, but she didn't know what she wanted to apologize for. For not caring? For not looking for her when she had the chance?

But Natalie had gotten away.

"Come inside," Natalie said when Rose still couldn't say anything.

Natalie led Rose through the little house and out the back, where a wooden porch sat before the jagged Montana mountains. Rose sat down as Natalie poured her a glass of iced tea. She then paused and gave Rose a look. "I might need something stronger," she confessed.

"I'd love anything you've got," Rose admitted.

Natalie returned with red wine from Napa and poured stiff glasses. She sat down and raised her glass. Rose told herself not to sob. She thought maybe she was dreaming.

Natalie's alive. This isn't a dream.

"I can't believe you got that guy behind bars," Natalie said.

Rose let out a laugh that turned into a sob. "It was his own fault," she said finally. "He made an error. He messed with my art." She swallowed. "He thought he could still mess with *me*, I guess. But I'm not the same as I was."

"It was only a matter of time before that idiot made a mistake," Natalie said.

Rose pressed her lips together. "You know, I bought your old house."

"I heard about that," Natalie said.

"How?"

"I read about it," Natalie said. "The news spits out stories about you and Oren and the Waldens every few minutes. Thank goodness I'm still labeled as 'dead.'" She laughed and shook her head.

"I can't believe he milked that sorrow about your death for so long," Rose said. "He knew you didn't die, obviously."

"What could he do? He had to pay someone off," Natalie said. "Otherwise, it looked like his wife just started a fire during an argument and ran out on him."

Rose swallowed. "That's what happened?"

Natalie nodded. "He was about to hit me. It's not like he hadn't done it before. I was so done. So exhausted. So when he wasn't looking—I think he was crying about how

I could never be the wife he really wanted—I set fire to the kitchen. Poof. It went up in flames."

"How did it happen so quickly?" Rose asked.

"I might have had some gasoline in the kitchen," Natalie said. "I might have planned the whole thing for weeks. I was just waiting for the time to strike."

Rose took a sip of wine. "You're the bravest woman I've ever met."

Natalie laughed. "I don't know about that. I had to completely abandon everything. I abandoned my name and my friends. It wasn't till a few weeks after my 'death' that I could contact my family and tell them I was safe. They totally freaked out, obviously. But we've been able to remain in contact all these years."

"When did you get to Montana?"

"It took a while," Natalie admitted. "I didn't have much money, and I had to pick up a few odd jobs here and there to get enough cash to come west. I figured Montana was perfect."

"He would never come out here," Rose agreed.

"Never."

They held the silence for a moment. Overhead, an eagle swooped, then perched in a tree that had to be one hundred feet tall.

"I met Graham when I was thirty-one," Natalie said. Graham was her husband; they owned the ranch together. "I didn't tell him what my real name was until about two years later. I was terrified. For some reason, I thought he was going to hit me. But he melted with sorrow. He held me in his arms and told me he would never let anything like that happen again." Natalie's tears came after that. She didn't bother to mop them up.

"I saw he'd married someone else," Natalie said. "I

hated how young you looked in your photograph in the paper. It broke my heart, knowing what he was going to do to you. But you got out."

"Eventually," Rose said.

"And you didn't even have to burn anything down," Natalie said.

Rose cast her gaze to the ground. "I don't know if I've ever really gotten over it."

Natalie took her hand on the table. "I'm always here to talk to you. I get it."

Rose pressed her lips together. She thought of Sean, waiting back in Nantucket for her. She thought about the tremendous density of the life she'd lived thus far. She raised her eyes to Natalie's and said, "There's life after Oren Grayson."

"So much of it," Natalie agreed. "I'm so grateful we had a chance to find it."

Coming Next in the Salt Sisters Series

Pre Order Before the Storm

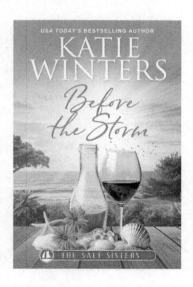

Other Books by Katie Winters

The Vineyard Sunset Series

Secrets of Mackinac Island Series

Sisters of Edgartown Series

A Katama Bay Series

A Mount Desert Island Series

A Nantucket Sunset Series

The Coleman Series

A Frosty Season Series

The Sutton Book Club Series

Connect with Katie Winters

Amazon
BookBub
Facebook
Newsletter

To receive exclusive updates from Katie Winters please
sign up to be on her Newsletter!
CLICK HERE TO SUBSCRIBE